Ashok K. Banker is the author of the internationally acclaimed Ramayana Series® and other books. He lives in Mumbai with his family. Visit him online at www.ashokbanker.com.

BOOKS BY ASHOK K. BANKER

Flute of Vrindavan

KRISHNA CORIOLIS — BOOK III

ASHOK K. BANKER

HARPER

First published in India in 2011 by Harper
An imprint of HarperCollins *Publishers*
a joint venture with
The India Today Group

Copyright © Ashok K. Banker 2011

ISBN: 978-93-5029-192-4

2 4 6 8 10 9 7 5 3 1

HarperCollins *Publishers*
A-53, Sector 57, Noida 201301, India
77-85 Fulham Palace Road, London W6 8JB, United Kingdom
Hazelton Lanes, 55 Avenue Road, Suite 2900, Toronto, Ontario M5R 3L2
and 1995 Markham Road, Scarborough, Ontario M1B 5M8, Canada
25 Ryde Road, Pymble, Sydney, NSW 2073, Australia
31 View Road, Glenfield, Auckland 10, New Zealand
10 East 53rd Street, New York NY 10022, USA

Typeset in 11.5/ 14.2 Adobe Jenson Pro
InoSoft Systems Noida

Printed and bound at
Thomson Press (India) Ltd.

For V.K. Karthika:
Editor, Publisher, Fellow Book Lover.
For helping baby Krishna take his first steps
and preparing the runway for his takeoff.
And for showing epic faith in me and my work.

All you faithful readers
who understand
that these tales
are not about being Hindu
or even about being Indian.
They're simply about being.

In that spirit,
I dedicate this gita-govinda
to the krishnachild in all of us.
For, under these countless
separate skins, there beats
a single eternal heart.

preface

If it takes a community to raise a child, it surely takes a nation to build an epic.

The itihasa of the subcontinent belongs to no single person. The great epics of our culture – of any culture – may be told and retold infinite times by innumerable poets and writers; yet, no single version is the final one.

The wonderful adventures of the great Lord Krishna are greater than what any story, edition or retelling can possibly encompass. The lila of God Incarnate is beyond the complete comprehension of any one person. We may each perceive some aspects of His greatness, but, like the blind men and the elephant, none of us can ever see everything at once.

It matters not whether you are Hindu or non-Hindu, whether you believe Krishna to be God or just a great historical personage, whether you are Indian or not. The richness and wonder of these tales have outlived countless generations and will outlast many more to come.

My humble attempt here – within these pages and in the volumes to follow – is neither the best nor the last retelling of this great story. I have no extraordinary talent or ability, no special skill or knowledge, no inner sight or visionary gift. What I *do* have is a lifelong exposure to an itihasa so vast, a culture so rich, a nation so great, wise and ancient, that their influence – permeating into one like water through peat over millennia, filtering through from mind to mind, memory to memory, mother to child and to mother again – has suffused every cell of my being, every unit of my consciousness.

And when I use the word 'I', it is meant in the universal. You are 'I'. As I am she. And she is all of us. Krishna's tale lives through each and every one of us. It is yours to tell. His to tell. Hers to tell. Mine as well. For as long as this tale is told, and retold, it lives on.

I have devoted years to the telling, to the crafting of words, sentences, paragraphs, pages, chapters, kaands and volumes. I shall devote more years to come, decades even. Yet, all my effort is not mine alone. It is the fruition of a billion Indians, and the billions who have lived before us. For each person who has known this tale and kept it alive in his heart has been a teller, a reteller, a poet, and an author. I am merely the newest name in a long, endless line of names that has had the honour and distinction of being associated with this great story.

It is my good fortune to be the newest reteller of this ancient saga. It is a distinction I share with all who tell and retell this story: from the grandmother who whispers it as a lullaby to the drowsy child, to the scholar who pores over each syllable of every shloka in an attempt to find an insight that has eluded countless scholars before him.

It is a tale told by me in this version; yet, it is not my tale alone to tell. It is your story. Our story. Her story. His story.

Accept it in this spirit and with all humility and hope. Also know that I did not create this flame, nor did I light the torch that blazes. I merely bore the torch this far. Now I give it to you. Take it from my hand. Pass it on. As it has passed from hand to hand, mind to mind, voice to voice, for unknown millennia.

Turn the page. See the spark catch flame.

Watch Krishna come alive.

author's note

All my books are long in the gestation, some conceived as many as thirty-plus years earlier, none less than a decade. It takes me that long to be sure of a story's longevity and worth and to accumulate the details, notes, research, character development and other tools without which I can't put my fingers to the keyboard. This particular story, Krishna Coriolis, originated in the same 'Big Bang' that was responsible for the creation of my entire Epic India universe – a series of interlinked retellings of all the major myths, legends and itihasa of the Indian subcontinent, set against the backdrop of world history. I'm using the term 'Big Bang' but in fact it was more of a series of carefully controlled delayed-time explosions over the first fifteen to eighteen years of my life.

At that time, the Krishna story was a part of the Sword of Dharma section of the Epic India library, which retold the 'dashavatara' storyline with an unusual twist as well as an integral part of my massively ambitious retelling of the world's greatest epic, the Mahabharata or the Mba. I began work on my Mba immediately after I completed the Ramayana Series in 2004. After about five years of working on my Mba – a period in which most actual MBA students would be firmly established in their careers! – I realized that the series was too massive to be published as it was. I saw that the Krishna storyline, in particular his individual adventures, could stand on their own as a separate series. So I separated them into a parallel series which I titled Krishna Coriolis. Naturally, since the story now had to stand on its own, rather than be a part of the larger Mba story, I had to rewrite each book to make it stand on its own, with a reasonably complete beginning, middle and end. This process took another three years, and resulted finally in the form the series now takes. You're holding the third book of this parallel series in your hands now, titled *Flute of Vrindavan*.

Flute of Vrindavan is just the third part of the Krishna Coriolis, which is interlinked with the much larger Mba series, which itself is only one section of my whole Epic India library. Yet, I've laboured to make this book stand on its own and be a satisfying read. Naturally, it's not complete in the story, since that would require not just the full Krishna storyline but also the larger Mba story and the larger context behind that as well. In that sense, it's just a part of the big picture; but even the longest journey must start with a single step and if you permit, *Flute of Vrindavan* will take you on a short but eventful trip, one packed with action and magic, terror and adventure. The reason why the book, like the remaining books in the series, is so short, almost half of the length of my earlier Ramayana Series, is because that's the best way the structure works. By that I mean the individual parts of the story and the way in which they fit together. Sure, I could make it longer – or shorter. But this felt like the perfect length. In an ideal world, the entire series would be packaged together as one massive book and published at once – but that's not only impossible in terms of paper thickness and binding and cover price affordability, it's not the right structure for the story. Stories have been split into sections, or volumes, or, in our culture, into parvas, kaands, suras, mandalas and so on, since literature was first written. You might as well ask the same question of Krishna Dweipayana-Vyasa – 'Sir, why did you split the Mahabharata into so many parvas and each parva into smaller sections and so on?' The fact is, a story needs to be structured and the story itself decides which structure works best. That was the case here and I am very pleased with the way *Flute of Vrindavan* and the other books in the series turned out.

The Sword of Dharma mini-series, as I call it now, is also written in first draft and tells us the experiences and adventures of Lord Vishnu in the heavenly realms. It is a direct sequel to the Ramayana Series as well as a bridge story to the Krishna Coriolis and Mahabharata Series. And since it deals with otherworldly events, it exists outside of 'normal' time as we know it, which means it is also a sequel to the Krishna Coriolis and also a prequel to the Ramayana Series. I won't confuse you further: once you read Sword of Dharma, you will understand what I mean because the story itself is an action-packed adventure story where questions like 'when is this taking place?' and 'so is this happening before or after such-and-such?' become less important than seeing the curtain parted and the world beyond the curtain revealed in its full glorious detail. No matter how much I may show you in the Ramayana Series, Krishna Coriolis and Mahabharata Series, all these 'mortal' tales are ultimately being affected and altered by events taking place at the 'immortal' level, and only by seeing that story-beyond-the-story can we fully comprehend the epic saga of gods and demons that forms the basis of Hindu mythology in our puranas.

But for now, *Flute of Vrindavan* marks a crucial turning point in the story of Swayam Bhagwan (as the Bhagwatham calls him). He has grown strong enough to fight the demonaic assassins sent by Kamsa, even as Kamsa has overcome his own obstacles and grown from strength to strength to challenge even the imperial ambitions of his venal father-in-law Jarasandha. The stage is set for the final showdown between God Incarnate and his nemesis. *Lord of Mathura*: Krishna Coriolis Book 4 will count down the pulse-pounding events and action-packaged adventures leading up to that climactic confrontation of nephew and uncle on the wrestling field in Mathura.

And that too is only part of the much, much larger tale of Krishna, which itself is part of the larger tale of Lord Vishnu, which is only part of the far greater saga of gods and demons. It's an epic saga, but the beauty of it is that each portion is delicious and fulfilling in itself!

Enjoy!

	yadrcchaya copapannah	
	svarga-dvaram apavrtam	
	sukhinah ksatriya partha	
	labhante yuddham idrsam	

Blessed are the warriors
Who are chosen to fight justly;
For the doors to heaven
Shall be opened unto them.

Kaand I

From far and wide they came. From every region of Vrajbhoomi, the Vrishnis arrived by uks cart, riding on bullocks or travelling on foot. Clad in their gaily coloured rustic apparel, driving their favourite kine along, chatting and singing and chanting aloud as they were wont to. Word of the amazing feat had spread within hours and before the end of the day, a great number of gopas and gopis had assembled to see for themselves if the amazing story contained any shred of truth. There were varying accounts of the incident, some barely resembling reality. Even the most honest descriptions sounded ludicrously exaggerated. A giantess? A demon of some kind? Slain by Nanda's and Yashoda's infant son? How could such a thing be possible? What was a giant demoness doing in Vrajbhoomi in the first place? How could a mere babe have killed her? By lengths and degrees the story grew until, by sunset, it had developed strands and twists to rival any epic. By nightfall the sutas were singing elaborate compositions describing the battle of the babe and the giantess!

'This is Lord Vishnu's blessing,' said Sumuka to his daughter and son-in-law. 'He is pleased with you for resisting the tyranny of the Usurper.' Like many Vrishnis, Yashoda's father preferred referring to the king of Mathura by that derogatory term rather than utter his vile name.

Yashoda and Nanda exchanged a meaningful glance. She raised her eyebrows questioningly. Barely perceptibly, he shook his head to answer in the negative. They had debated whether or not to reveal their infant son's extraordinary nature to their family and friends, but had decided against it. Whatever the child did openly, they could not cover up. There was no need to cover it up: people would invariably attribute every miraculous action to the blessings of some deity or the other. But once they voiced aloud their belief that their son was something more than human, perhaps even touched with a trace of divinity himself, people's perception of their son would change completely. Word would spread like wildfire and soon enough everyone across the kingdom would know about it. Including the Usurper. And while they already knew that their little tyke was possessed of great power, they had no wish to test the limits of his abilities and invite the terror of Mathura to come and attempt to slay him. Whatever he might be, he was but a boy. And he was *their* boy. Empowered or no, there would be time enough for him to reveal the full extent of his abilities to the world, or not, as he pleased. It would not have been wise for them to boast about it there and then, not when Mathura's spasas were everywhere, watching, listening, still seeking the prophesied Slayer. Putana had been one such spasa; they knew that now. And what a creature she had been! Seemingly quite normal, she had turned out to be a demoness of some sort. Something out of puranic tales and legends, a rakshasi perhaps. Who knew what other demons were lurking nearby, seeking their chance to attack the purported child of the prophecy. No, they had both agreed in the moments following Putana's death – when they had regrouped and consulted with each other before their clansmen began arriving in force – that it was wiser to simply pretend to know nothing and let people draw their own conclusions.

And the conclusion drawn was the inevitable one: God's grace.

'Vishnu has protected this child!' reckoned Dadhisara, and she was echoed in turn by a hundred others. Everyone had the same thought, and that was so much better. Better that they believed it was the Great Preserver who had protected their child in his moment of crisis than that the babe himself was some superior being.

Then followed the inevitable rituals of the Vrishnis after such an event. Rare though such events were, attacks by demons upon mortals were not unheard of. Whether corporeal or ethereal, it was believed that asuras were everywhere in some form or the other, attempting ceaselessly to attack and destroy the righteous. The Vrishnis, like all other Sura Yadava clans, had specific rituals designed to ward off such attacks.

First, all the gopis of Gokul formed a protective circle around little Krishna. He giggled and turned around to look at the pretty young girls and women standing around him, regarding it as some kind of game. Still unsteady on his chubby feet, he swayed constantly, and Yashoda kept wanting to dart out her hands to grab him before he fell, but somehow he always managed to retain his balance. He danced around, looking at all the gopis, pointing at the prettier ones as if approving of them, then stuffing the back of his fist into his mouth and sucking on it noisily. His antics amused them all and the gopis were entranced by the way he moved and danced.

They took up the same chant they had sung earlier, when he had danced upon the corpse of the giantess. Since everyone else had arrived too late to fully comprehend what had happened, it was assumed that somehow the demoness had been stricken down by Vishnu's power and fallen down dead, and the infant Krishna, saved by God's grace, had then taken his first steps upon her corpse. Even those who had witnessed the dance of Govinda found themselves unable to fully comprehend that it was Krishna himself who had slain her, and Yashoda was glad that Nanda and she had decided to keep that crucial fact to themselves. For who would believe that an infant could slay a great demoness? Or for that matter, how had Krishna killed her? All she had seen was him clinging to the demoness's breast, suckling. It had appeared as if he was sucking the very life out of her. But was that what had happened? She had no way of knowing for certain. It was as if a miasma obscured that part of her memory – and the memory of the others who had witnessed the event. Perhaps that was how Hari desired it. So it was best to remain silent and let people believe what they did: that Vishnu himself had looked down and intervened to save the son of Yashoda-devi and Nanda Maharaja.

'Govinda! Govinda! Govinda!' chanted the gopis. The word simply meant 'cowherd', but it was also a title of sorts, accorded to a young boy when he proved himself able enough to herd the cows of his family or clan, protect them from inclement weather or wild beasts, and bring them home safe. Govinda was also the universal term for the Celestial Cowherd who herded all cattle and kine everywhere, and therefore was a deity to cowherds everywhere. The term also had a playful connotation, for among the Vrishni, Govindas played as they worked, flirting, making music, dancing, feasting and doing as they willed. To apply the title to an infant who had barely begun walking was high praise indeed. As the whole community watched and sang along,

Yashoda felt herself flush with pride at the sight of her son being called by the esteemed title.

'Govinda! Govinda! Govinda!' sang the gopis and little Krishna laughed and danced round and round, clapping his hands unsteadily, sometimes missing and almost losing his balance – but quickly regaining it and resuming his lurching dance.

One of the gopis, an attractive woman named Shyamolie, came forward holding a cow by its tail. She waved it around Krishna as he danced, encircling him. The tips of the cowtail tickled Krishna's ears and neck and he giggled and squirmed. Looking up at the object that had stimulated him, he tried to grasp it, but Shyamolie kept it out of his reach. He laughed, with his eyes fixed unblinkingly at the tail hanging right above his head, and tried to spin, slowly, and then faster, to grab it. Yashoda saw that he could spin as rapidly as a top – or as the wind itself – if he desired, and she caught her breath, afraid that the gopis would witness the superhuman side of her little tyke. But Shyamolie ceased waving the cowtail and retired and Krishna slowed down. Yashoda heaved a sigh, smiling with relief.

Then came the bathing of the child in cow's urine. This part Krishna ought not to have enjoyed as much as the chanting and dancing, but he endured it stoically, even slapping himself and splashing the urine on the faces of the gopis who were bathing him. They laughed, undeterred. All products of goumata were sacred and to be revered; there was no shame in being splashed with cow urine.

Next came the sprinkling of cow dust – literally the dust from the dried cow dung – on the child. This left Krishna's dark bluish-black skin powdery brown for a while. He beamed brightly at his mother as if to say: 'Not to worry, I'm fine, Maatr.' She was glad he did not speak to her mind just then; she might not have been able to avoid reacting in front of so many people.

Then came the writing of the names of the Preserver. Using fingertips dipped in wet cow dung, twelve different names of Vishnu were written on twelve different parts of Krishna's body – the forehead; throat; chest; the centre, left and right sides of the belly; left and right shoulders; left and right biceps; top and bottom of the back.

As Yashoda watched from behind the circle of busy gopis, she saw each name glow from within as it was written, as if Krishna's skin had reacted to the shape of the letters. The glow was very faint and only visible if you were staring directly at that spot at that instant: the gopis were too busy writing the next name to notice. So only she saw this subtle effect. But it was unmistakeable in its power and meaning. Each name glowed briefly, its colour a distinct deep blue, then dissipated inwards. It was as if the names were being absorbed into the bloodstream of her son, leaving only the shapeless crusted cow dung on the skin. She swallowed and looked around, wishing she could share this new evidence of her son's extraordinary nature with someone; then reminded herself it was for the best that his true nature be kept a secret.

It was ironic though, she mused, that the gopis were invoking the protection of Vishnu upon one who was empowered as Vishnu himself!

The gopis then sprinkled sacred water – brought from the Yamuna –over their bodies, and applied the bija seed mantra to themselves, invoking the first syllable of the deity's name followed by the nasal 'nam' sound. Then they applied the same bija seed mantra to Krishna who gurgled happily and raised his arms in the air.

The gopis chanted:

|May the Unborn One protect your feet|
|Maniman, protect your knees|
|Yajna, protect your thighs|
|Achyuta, protect your loins|
|Hayasa, protect your belly|
|Kesava, protect your heart|
|Isa, protect your chest|
|Ina, protect your throat|
|Vishnu, protect your arms|
|Urukrama, protect your mouth|
|Isvara, protect your head|
|The wielder of the chakra, protect your forebody|
|Hari who wields the bala, protect your rearbody|
|Madhu-slayer and the Unborn One|
|Bearer of the bow and the sword|
|Protect your sides|
|Urugaya, conch-blower, protect your corners|
|Upendra, protect you from above|
|Tarksya, protect you on the ground|
|The Supreme One, plough-pusher, protect you on all sides|
|Hrishikesha, protect your senses|
|Narayana, protect your life force|
|The Lord of Shvetadvipa, protect your consciousness|
|Lord of yoga, protect your mind|
|Prshnigarbha, protect your intelligence|
|Bhagwan Supreme, protect your soul|
|Govinda, protect you at play|

|Madhava, protect you while you sleep|
|Vaikuntha, protect you when you travel|
|Lord of the goddess of good fortune, protect you while
 you are seated still|
|Enjoyer of sacrifices and terror of all evil spirits, protect
 you while you eat|

In conclusion, they chanted verses designed to chase away any of the evil beings known to abduct or harm infants, such as the dakinis, yatudhanis, kusmandas, bhoot-preyt, pisachas, yaksas, rakshasas, vinayakas, Kotara, Revati, Jyestha, Putana, the Maatrakas, insane persons, those who have lost their senses or memories, they who seek to harm humans, the old enemies of humankind, snatchers of children and every other imaginable being that might cause harm to little Krishna.

By the time the gopis were done, even Krishna was tired. He had curled up and gone to sleep sucking the back of his fist, and had to be carried indoors by his mother. She fed him from her breast till he was sated enough to fall asleep with the teat still in his puckered wet lips.

He then proceeded to sleep soundly for a full night and the whole of the next morning.

Perhaps, Yashoda thought to herself, *even the divine in mortal form is subject to weaknesses and the limitations of mortal flesh. He may be empowered beyond imagining but he is still a human babe. He still tires, needs sleep, nourishment, rest, and is subject to all the bodily functions and needs of the mortal being whose form he has chosen to adopt. If a deva resides in a tree, he must grow roots and leaves and would need sunlight and water. If residing in a babe, he needs milk and sleep and laughter and love!*

She slept with him cradled in the warmth of her embrace. Mother and son slept soundly and peacefully. Nanda came often to check on them and a guard was maintained around the clock to ensure that nobody came within harming distance of the mother and infant.

Kamsa listened to the spasa's report. When the spy had finished, he dismissed him and sat brooding for a while. His ministers approached him several times, saw him sitting in that familiar meditative posture – chin resting on fist, arm supported by thigh – and retreated quickly. As the minutes dragged on, they began whispering in the palace corridors, speculating on the news that had disturbed their king so deeply. 'Putana,' was the consensus. 'He has taken the news of her loss to heart.' And the spasa, when waylaid and questioned, agreed readily: his news had been mainly of Putana's death in distant Gokuldham. Nobody knew exactly what Putana had been to Kamsa – friend, advisor, training partner, lover, mistress, all of these, none of these … Nobody knew enough to speak confidently. And those who did know something, had perhaps glimpsed the king and the captain's wife speaking with odd passion and intense gestures in the stables and training field, knew better than to spread idle gossip about the king of Mathura. Thousands had been slaughtered for reasons much more trivial under the young lord's reign. To be hauled up for gossiping about his indiscretions would surely merit torture of unimaginable cruelty. So they whispered and speculated, in corners and hallways, in half-sentences and incomplete queries, nobody saying much at all, leaving almost everything to the imagination and to curiosity. But one thing was certain, undeniable: Kamsa was stricken by the news of Putana's death. Stricken to the core.

After perhaps an hour of sitting and fretting alone in the throne room, Kamsa rose and left the chamber. Voices in the corridors hushed at once as the imposing young liege swept past, his gold-brocaded robes swirling in his wake. His handsome, clean and smooth face was a porcelain mask with no expression. His fair features and handsome light eyes wore a fixed aspect that none had seen before.

Now he walked into the great court which fell silent as he entered. Those seated were all members of the inner circle of power. Ministers and courtiers and munshis who had survived the ten terrible years since Ugrasena's unseating. They were well-weathered veterans who had seen the young king in every mood, through every change. On any other day, they could recognize his moods and his likely reactions – even as a rakshasa, during his awful gargantuan puss-suppurating phase, and as a violent rage-prone youth during his years of cruel and mindless slaughter. But this new Kamsa was an inscrutable being. He was normal and human in all aspects, behaved and spoke normally, even conducted himself with rare self-control and aplomb in the most provocative situations. It was commonly accepted that Jarasandha's prolonged stay had something to do with the transformation. The emperor of the burgeoning Magadhan Empire had hammered some sense of good conduct into his son-in-law's thick skull, it seemed. What was more surprising was that Kamsa's good behaviour continued even after Jarasandha's departure. And at times like this, if he felt or thought anything intensely, he did not show or share it with anyone. For an Arya king, especially a Yadava, such extreme self-control was unnatural, almost inhuman. It was one thing to control oneself from flying into a rage and mindlessly slaughtering thousands for no good reason, but another to withhold *all* one's emotions from public scrutiny. Yadavas were passionate, open-hearted people. Even their kings displayed emotion freely, laughing and crying in public if the occasion warranted. In this context, Kamsa's inscrutability was no less unnerving than his earlier rakshasa rages. If too much emotional reaction was demoniac, too little was inhuman.

Kamsa swept past all the curious and concerned in his court without a word or indication as to what he was feeling or planning. Watched by a hundred pairs of eyes, he left the main palace and walked across the courtyard to his own quarters. Even after Jarasandha's departure, he had elected to remain in the relatively modest and remotely situated apartments at the far end of the palace complex, unguarded and within scent of the stables and pens. In fact, on his own instructions, no palace personnel were permitted to come within a hundred yards of his private quarters, on pain of death. If nobody had been arrested or executed for transgressing this instruction, it was only because nobody dared try. Besides, who would want to go near Kamsa's quarters? People wanted to be as far away from him as they could! He was, after all, the king under whose reign a mass exodus of Yadavas had taken place. The largest emigration in the history of the Yadava nation. Apart from the old warrior Bahuka and the captain of the guards, Pradyota, nobody had even been inside those private apartments, nor did anyone wish to go there. Except Putana, of course. Or so it was rumoured.

Kamsa did not stop at his residence. He continued walking past the entrance, past the pens where all manner and species of livestock chattered and clucked and thrashed and howled and bayed and lunged as he strode past. He went straight to the stables, took hold of the first horse he saw and climbed astride it. The horse was one of the large Bhoja giants that were bred specially for him. Enormous in comparison to the pony-sized horses usually used by Yadavas, it was well over two yards high at the withers, and the tips of its ears were three full yards from the ground. Like the others in this section of the stables, it had been bred for bone density and strength, fed on a special diet, and put through a special training regime usually used to train elephants to carry heavy timber loads. It was assumed by the other trainers that the horses in this stable were being trained to carry some newfangled Magadhan armour which was so strong that it could withstand even a flung javelin. What other reason could there be to breed such enormous unruly giants and prepare them to carry loads of a half-ton or more? None of the other trainers would venture near this stable because the horses here were ungelded and so ferocious at times, it was beyond the ability of any man to control them and survive. Only the ancient trainer, the one who had been at the stables since before anyone else could remember, and who was rumoured to be one of the oldest living Mathurans, manned the stable – on his own. Aptly enough, he was named Yadu, after the founding father of the Yadava race.

Yadu was in the stables when Kamsa entered and took hold of a horse. The ancient syce stopped mucking out the stables and lowered his rake to watch as the young king led the rearing, snorting horse outside. Then he put down the rake and went out as well, through the other entrance at the far end of the stables.

Yadu watched as Kamsa manipulated the reluctant stallion up to the fenced enclosure that bordered the stable yard. The horse was clearly making its displeasure known and was bucking and pulling away from the king though Kamsa had it by a rope through his nostrils. The young king managed the horse with apparent ease until he turned his back for a moment to untie and push open the gate of the enclosure. The horse saw its opportunity and struck: rearing up to a height of four yards or more, towering above even the tall and powerfully built king of Mathura, the stallion lashed out viciously with its forefeet. Yadu had seen the same horse smash those same forefeet through an inch-thick siding of wood a fortnight ago but the old Yadava's deeply wrinkled face did not flinch as the stallion struck Kamsa on his back and shoulders. Any other man, however muscular or strong, would have been thrown several yards away with shattered bones and serious contusions.

The horse's feet landed on Kamsa's back and shoulders – the right forefoot actually struck directly on his collarbone – with a sound that reminded old Yadu of a mace striking a tree. Mace warriors sometimes practised that way, striking their weapons into the trunks of massive trees to prepare themselves for the impact of combat. The living wood absorbed enough of the impact so as not to dislocate their shoulders or harm their joints and bones, yet withstood it strongly enough to provide good conditioning to the limbs. A dull metallic thud. Not the cracking of bone or the slapping sound of flesh being traumatized.

Kamsa remained standing.

He barely lurched a little, perhaps an inch or two forward, not even enough to consider it a jolt or a jostle.

Then he turned and looked at the horse. The stallion was still rearing, eyes showing white, nostrils flared, whinnying in that triumphant tone that male horses used when they had proven their superiority over a fellow equine or a two-legged human.

Kamsa tugged down the rope with which he held the horse.

The stallion's forepaws crashed down on the ground, as if yanked by a ton-weight. Its eyes rolled and it almost buckled from the impact.

Kamsa had barely used any force to pull at the horse; he had tugged a finger's length perhaps, casually. He seemed to bear no malice towards the horse for having struck him.

He kicked open the untied gate, which shattered into fragments. Then he led the horse into the enclosure. He turned, grasped hold of the horse's neck and leapt astride.

The horse lurched, shuddering as if a man twice Kamsa's size and bearing the heaviest armour had leapt onto its back from a height.

Kamsa steadied it, used the slender length of rope to turn its head, then pressed in his heels to urge it forward.

The horse began to ride around the enclosure.

Kamsa slapped it on the rump, urging it to go faster, still faster.

The horse shook its head from side to side, protesting, eyes still showing their whites, clearly still unable to comprehend how the human had survived that blow from its powerful forepaws. Most other men – indeed, *any* other man – would be lying on the ground with a shattered collarbone and a smashed shoulder blade, not to mention collapsed lungs and perhaps even a damaged spine. It was a killing blow and intended as such. Yet Kamsa had barely felt it.

The horse on the other hand had definitely felt Kamsa when he climbed astride. And the slap on the rump. And the heels he was now digging into its flanks to urge it to go faster.

Yadu saw the furrows.

The horse was riding around the large enclosure. It had just completed one circle and was about to go over its own hoofprints again.

The ungulate footprints in the ground ought not to have been particularly noticeable. The ground was fairly solid and dry for the most part and where it was softer, it had been churned up by the hooves of any number of horses. The stallion's prints should have been mixed up in the general pattern.

Instead, they stood out as clearly as a furrow drawn by a plough.

They were shallow and almost normal at the beginning, where Kamsa had begun his ride. But as Yadu glanced quickly around the enclosure, he saw the prints grow steadily deeper and wider until finally, by the time the stallion came around to complete the first circle, the hoofprints were inches deep, so deep that the ground was being furrowed by its passage. And as it thundered past, Yadu could feel the impact through the ground. It felt as if a half-score horses were carrying as many heavy men riding hard and fast.

Yet even a half-score mounted horses could not make furrows that deep. Because even they probably did not weigh as much as this one, with only Kamsa on its back.

Yadu watched as the stallion carried Kamsa around for the second time. This time the hooves were sinking so deep into the ground, the old man could see them buried up to the fetlocks before they emerged and ploughed ahead. The horse was straining impossibly to carry its unbearable load, its youth, virility and inbred pride enhancing its natural obduracy to the point of folly. Its head jerked upwards with each forward movement, its nostrils flared, eyes rolled up to reveal almost all white, and its hooves were furrowing through the ground like a plough-blade, throwing up masses of sods. Kamsa sat calmly on its back, doing nothing more than urging it forward. The horse made one final tremendous effort, then collapsed. The sound of it falling to the ground beneath Kamsa was exactly like that of a young sapling cracked by a powerful mace blow, and on hearing it, Yadu did wince, for while he cared little about what happened to Kamsa himself, he cared greatly about the animals under his care. The horse collapsed like a deflated leather bladder, its legs snapping like twigs immediately after its great back broke, and lay crumpled in a defeated heap.

It had taken only one-and-a-half rounds of the enclosure and a few minutes for Kamsa to destroy a horse that could carry almost as much weight as a young cow elephant.

And all he had done was ride it.

Kamsa leapt off the back of the horse. The impact of his feet hitting the ground was audible all the way across the enclosure to where Yadu stood. A thumping sound. And when he strode away, Yadu could make out the imprints of his feet even from the distance at which he stood. Those footprints were inches deep in the hard-packed ground.

Kamsa walked away without even a glance at Yadu. But the old syce knew that he was aware of his presence. He had seen Kamsa in such a state before, although never so enraged. For despite the inscrutability and lack of ranting, shouting or other typical signs of anger, Yadu knew it was pure rage that fuelled Kamsa. Ever since his secret training under Putana's guidance, Ugrasena's son had changed his very personality; gone was the Kamsa of yore who threw people out of windows and slaughtered infants. In his place was this Kamsa, a being who distilled all his rage into a cold, relentless, unstoppable juggernaut and went on rampages that would have left swathes of bloody enemy dead had it been a battlefield.

At such times, Yadu knew, the young king withdrew into himself, compacting his consciousness until he appeared to be aware of nothing but his own existence, seeing, hearing, feeling nothing but what transpired within his inscrutable mind. But he was guarded by a survival instinct so powerful that not so much as an ant could attempt to nip at his toe without him being aware of the attempt before it could occur. Yadu knew that Kamsa had known of the young horse rearing up to crush him, and that he was aware of him standing there, watching. He knew also that he was the only human being alive that Kamsa permitted to witness him at such a time, doing such things, and still let live.

Apart from Putana, of course.

Kamsa made his way towards the far fence of the enclosure. The gate on that side was several score yards away. Kamsa did not bother to walk towards the gate, untie it, open it, and walk through. Instead, he simply strode through the fence itself. The inch-thick wooden planks, designed to withstand the powerful kicks of rebellious stallions and strong mares in heat, shattered into splinters. He walked through half-a-dozen fences in similar manner, striding across the length of the training field, and by the time he had reached the far end, the trail of his footprints resembled the wake of a plough.

Kamsa began running as he approached the woods at the far side of the training field, running with the heavy gait of an overly muscled man though he was fairly slender and well-shaped. He moved as if running through wet sand, his feet churning as much as a foot's depth of earth as he gained pace.

He brushed against the trunk of a sala tree just before he disappeared into the woods, and a chunk of the tree was torn out of its body to land on the ground. The tops of trees shuddered visibly, and great clumps of birds rose up in alarm and flew wheeling over the woods, crying out in dismay.

Then the woods settled back to normal, and Kamsa was gone from sight.

three

Nanda and the gopas undertook the task of disposing of Putana's body. They used wood axes to chop up the body into pieces. The task was unpleasant but not as much as they had expected: the body exuded no fluids, blood or otherwise, and instead of the usual stench of dead flesh, it gave off a pleasant aroma. This confounded the Vrishnis until Guru Gargamuni said that it was a sign that the demoness had attained moksha in death and ascended. This elicited further looks of wonderment from all present, for it confirmed their conviction that God had played a direct hand in saving little Krishna's life. Being slain by a god was itself one way of achieving salvation from the eternal cycle of birth and death, freedom from karma – and the perfumed odour and bloodless body of the giantess indicated that she had not merely perished but had been released.

This made their task less onerous and they went about the grisly work with grim satisfaction. Mounting the pieces onto wagons, they carted the remains to a distant ghat where they piled them with wood and burned them piece by piece, ensuring that not a scrap was left for carrion birds or vermin to feed on. Even the smoke rising from the remains gave off a pleasant smell. It was Nanda's elder brother Upananda who identified the fragrance. 'Aloe!' he said, 'it smells like aloe.' And so it did, Sannanda, their younger brother agreed, and even Nandana, the youngest of the four brothers, concurred. They had been concerned about the vile ash and smoke travelling to fields and being inhaled by cattle but now they knew that there was not a trace of the demon left on earth. Vishnu had ensured that the act of death was also one of purification.

When every last vestige of Putana was consigned to flame, ash and smoke, they returned to Nanda's house. Yashoda was caught up in the usual hustle and bustle of catering to and caring for the needs of so many guests and barely had time to think about the horrendous event. It was only much later, when she was alone in her cot with little Krishna by her side, sleeping on his back, limbs sprawled in that unique way only the very young can manage, that she was overcome briefly by a surge of anxiety.

What if there are others? If Kamsa sent one assassin, surely he will send more! What if the next one is too powerful to overcome? What if harm comes to my little one?

More than anything else, she knew that so long as Kamsa lived, there would be no real peace for her or her little son. The ruthless usurper would never cease in his attempts.

This time, there was no mind voice from her little Krishna speaking to her and reassuring her as before. He seemed to be sleeping more soundly than usual. That itself indicated that he was exhausted from the encounter with Putana and suggested there were limits to his abilities or to his endurance. After all, he was still a little babe.

Overcome with anxiety, for the first time, Yashoda wished – nay, she *longed* – for her little one to speak to her and calm her fears.

But Krishna slept on, soundly, even snoring a little.

It was with a troubled heart that Yashoda finally lulled herself to sleep.

four

Kamsa increased his pace as he emerged from the woods north-west of Mathura. This region was dry unforested land, too barren to farm and too hostile to inhabit. The ground suddenly gave way to plunging gulches here, many of them dangerously steep and narrow. The streams at the bottom of those steep gulches were barely muddy trickles and most were bone dry, carpeted with the bones of animals that had fallen to their deaths. They only filled up during the monsoon and a few weeks thereafter. The area was too uncertain for habitation and had as a result been overrun by predators. Kamsa went there to practise his newfound abilities daily, testing the limits of his transformed body, exploring the possibilities, developing his unusual skills further, finding new ways to use them for combat. There was a particular box canyon he had favoured at first. But he had long since demolished it and reduced it to a heap of rubble. Later, under Putana's supervision, he had developed a regime that catered to his particular abilities and strengths. But on that particular day, following a daily regime was the last thing on his mind.

Feet pounding up chunks of earth, he simply ran, stomping noisily, leaving a dust trail bigger than that left by a herd of stampeding elephants. The ground shuddered beneath his increasing weight. The rage and anguish that filled his heart were unbearable. He could not resist expressing them any longer.

Putana is dead.

His first friend in years, his only female companion, his only genuine advisor, the one person he had come to rely on, to seek solace in, who comforted him and made him feel ... almost human. The only one who had understood him, his strange urges and impulses, his abilities and enormous power, his rakshasa lusts and human longings. Gone. And only after she was gone did he realize how much she had truly meant to him.

She had loved him and he had loved her, in a manner of speaking. As much as a being such as she and a rakshasa-mortal hybrid such as he could actually love anyone.

Whatever he was, she had accepted him fully and had befriended him, coming closer to him than anyone else he had ever known. She was a maatr: one of a great ancient coven of Mother-Creators, demigods who had been present during the creation of the world, she had taken shelter among mortals and disguised her true form and power in order to survive and to atone for past transgressions. She had fed Kamsa the Halahala – a deadly toxin capable of slaying humans with a single drop, and which to him, with his newly reconstituted biology, was an elixir and tonic – from her own body. This act had made them bond powerfully.

Now he would no longer have her milk to give him new strength each day. But more importantly, he would no longer have her strength of character, her great ancient wisdom and insight, her knowledge of so many things that he could barely comprehend. It was she who had refused to let him confront the Slayer. He had wanted to go the instant she brought him word that the Slayer had been traced at last. He had wanted to go at once and face his nemesis. The child of his sister who had miraculously survived his decade-long campaign. The

prophesied one who would some day kill him, Kamsa, and take
his place upon the throne of Mathura. He had wanted to go
and crush that little tyke with a single swing of his mighty fist.
But Putana had stopped him, had told him that he was not yet
ready, not strong enough to face the Slayer.

Not strong enough! Hah!

She was very persuasive and had chosen to go instead, and to
use her deadly toxic milk to kill the Slayer. She said it was the
best way. He had agreed then because it did seem ingenious. The
Slayer was but an infant. Were he, Kamsa, to go and kill him,
it would provoke the people again. No longer were they quiet
and subordinate to his atrocities as they had been at first. The
stench of rebellion was in the air. Such an act of outright murder
might have brought all the Vrishnis and Suras against him in
one massive civil action. Putana's way was more sensible, he had
to admit. She would simply go and nurse the infant, feeding him
the most toxic substance in Creation. Nobody would suspect
Kamsa. His hands would be clean.

But now Putana herself was dead!

Her plan had failed. Kamsa did not know the details – what
he knew was what the dhoot, the spasa–courier, had told him:
a giant demoness of some kind had been killed by an infant in
Gokuldham. The infant had danced on her corpse after killing
her.

Danced!

It was believed that the giantess was named Putana. The
spy had not even known it was Kamsa's Putana, the wife of the
captain of his guard; he had merely reported what he had heard
in Gokuldham. But Kamsa had known at once. Putana was
dead. She had attempted to slay the nursling and had herself

been slain. She was gone. And he was alone once more. And he could not bear it.

He was approaching the edge of a gulch, and was running too fast to stop. Even if he slowed, his weight and momentum would carry him off the edge. So, instead of bothering to stop or slow down, he ran faster. He launched himself off the edge of a ravine several hundred feet high. The far side was a good fifty yards away. He flew up into the air, wreathed in a dust cloud, and as he hung suspended over certain death for any mortal flesh, he beat his chest and roared his anguish to the skies.

The sound echoed through the ravine below his flailing feet.

His momentum carried him all the way across to the far ridge. He landed in an explosion of dust and shale, cracking the stony back of the ledge. A small avalanche's worth of debris collapsed behind him into the abyss. But he was already racing away, across dry, almost desert-bare terrain, his body so heavy now that his feet were embedded a whole yard deep in the surface of the ground. He tore up earth and rocks and roots and stones the way a chariot's wheels might throw up clods of supple soil. He barely felt his thighs ploughing through solid ground and stone with greater ease than a metal plough blade could churn through sodden earth. He felt his power, his strength, his invulnerability. It was a palpable thing, as real as the air pumping in and out of his lungs, the sunlight on his face, the scent of freshly broken earth in his nostrils. He felt the very cells of his body resist the onslaught of stone and earth as he tore through the ground, and at that moment he knew that there were no limits to his power. He only needed to learn how to control his body, to focus long and hard enough to increase his density to the point he desired, and he could become strong enough to punch through stone if required, or withstand any force and survive unharmed. The only problem was focussing so intensely and holding his concentration long enough. But he would master that as well. He would grow stronger than ever before, stronger than anything or anyone else on earth. He would do it for Putana. To avenge her. By slaying the one who had slain her.

He slowed as he saw something ahead. Something alive and mobile.

He came to a halt, the dust cloud settling slowly around him and the long winding trail of furrowed ground stretching for a mile and more in his wake. He stared at the moving shapes ahead, milling about in confusion and hostility as they sensed the strange being that had intruded unexpectedly.

It was a herd of rhinoceros. It was unusual for them to be seen together as they were mostly solitary creatures. But he did not question or think about the why or wherefore. He looked at them and they stared at him suspiciously, lowering their horns, stamping their feet and snorting threateningly, warning him to stay away. They had younguns. That meant they would fight to the death to protect them.

All Kamsa cared about was that they would provide him an outlet.

Humans were insufficient: there was no sport in being able to smash soft bags of pulpy flesh and brittle bone. It was like a boy mashing insects between his thumb and forefinger – as he himself had done when he was a boy.

He needed some real sport. Something that would offer opposition, could withstand his iron blows and stone flesh.

Rhinoceros. What could be better?

He grinned, baring an inane smile in a reddened face.

Then he began running straight towards the herd. The rhinos snorted in surprise, lowering their horns and charging at him. He charged back. There were four of them rushing towards him at the same time, all large adult rhinoceroses. The two smaller ones stayed back, making sounds of distress; an adult female stayed with them.

Man-rakshasa and rhinos thundered at each other with the fury of creatures that were supremely confident that nothing could withstand their onslaught.

Kamsa had seen rhinos charge at solid wooden walls inches thick and drive their horns through them like nails through soft wood. He had seen them smash human bodies to mangled pulp in Jarasandha's sports arenas, had witnessed them knock down elephants and pound stone walls until they cracked and shook. He knew the damage these creatures could inflict when enraged or challenged. By challenging them so when they were with their young, he was invoking their greatest fury. They would not rest now until he was dead.

Unfortunately for them, the rhinos had no idea of the damage Kamsa could inflict.

Two-legged being and four-legged creatures met in a thumping impact.

When the dust cleared, two rhinos were lying on their sides in the dirt, bleeding profusely, their horns shattered. The other two milled about in confusion, unable to fathom what had happened. Never before in their lives had they encountered a living creature that could withstand their direct charge.

Arms on his hips, Kamsa stood facing them, grinning. He was happy now. Still enraged at Putana's loss, but happier than he had been a few moments ago. He had killed – or at the very least inflicted mortal wounds – upon living beings. That was the one thing that could always elevate his mood. Happiness was an opponent best served dead.

He charged towards the rhinos again.

And again.

And again.

When all four adults were dead, their armour-plated bodies lying broken and bleeding from a dozen wounds, heads and horns torn and ripped and mangled from the terrible impact, he turned to the surviving adult female and the two younguns. They were bleating in distress but still lowering their horns and stamping their feet, ready to defend themselves to the death.

He was happy to oblige them.

He charged again. And again. Until there was not a living rhino left.

After that, he felt happier.

And that is how he mourned the death of Putana.

five

Nanda was worried. If he failed to express his anxieties to his wife, it was because he did not want to alarm Yashoda any further. But he had received word from Akrur to beware of assassins from Mathura. And the group of travellers that had accompanied Lady Putana to Gokuldham had mysteriously disappeared around the time of her death. Nobody in Gokul had seen them leaving, and their belongings had vanished from the quarters he had assigned to them. It was extremely worrying. It was now evident that all of them had been sent to his house on a nefarious mission. What were their names? He could remember the names of only three of the several courtiers who accompanied Putana: Agha, Baka and Trnavarta, and he felt little satisfaction in doing so. No doubt they had gone underground by now, altering their appearance and garb. For all he knew, they could be mingling with the Vrishnis, pretending to be gopas!

But what made him truly anxious was the sight of Putana's enormous body. That elegant noblewoman, wife of the captain of the Mathura guard, no less, a woman of high birth who had been known in Mathura aristocracy even before Kamsa had dethroned his father and installed himself as king – if she could turn out to be such a terrible demoness, who knew what other demons might lurk in Mathura or across the Yadava nation? It was frightening, though, to accept that there were demons living

among them, seemingly human in every respect, until the day
they set forth on a particular mission. In this case, to assassinate
an infant child! And the three other visitors had been former
aides of the God Emperor Jarasandha of Magadha, who was
himself rumoured to be the most powerful demon of all; there
was no doubt they were empowered with asura maya as well.
He could not begin to think where or how they might strike at
his little son.

How to protect Krishna was the most daunting question of
all. He could hardly surround Yashoda and their son with lathi-
armed guards night and day. It would invade his wife's privacy
and be preposterous. She would never have a moment alone and
the presence of the guards would make her anxious and rob her
of all peace. He knew his beloved wife well. She believed that
carrying a sword was itself an invitation to violence.

So he set several of his most trusted gopas and gopis to keep
a discreet watch. He recruited family – Yashoda's brothers and
sisters as well as his own – among this number too. This way, she
would see familiar beloved faces surround her and take comfort
in their presence, while their mission would be to watch over
her and send for the real guards the instant they sensed danger.
The armed guards would be kept at bay – out of Yashoda's
sight but within quick hailing distance – and would operate in
shifts and be on alert every moment of the day or night. Nanda
received more volunteers for this duty than he required. Then
again, how many were too many? If a giantess attacked again,
would it take ten armed men to bring her down? Or forty? Or
a hundred? Who knew what powers the other assassins might
possess or how they would attack!

Still, all he could do was prepare and anticipate, and he did.

He offered to pay the volunteers for the time spent away from their own herds but they would not hear of it. They readily agreed to drink his famous Gokul milk and consume its products, though! That was payment enough, they said, brushing milk off their elaborate moustaches with the backs of their hands, grinning.

So began a routine of Yashoda and Nanda pretending that all was normal, smiling, laughing, talking, going about their daily chores, meeting and receiving people, doing everything they used to do before. However, the normalcy was tainted by the pallor of fear hanging over them, and it dampened everything they did. Nanda could see it clearly: Yashoda would be talking with her sisters and friends and notice some stranger approach Krishna, and her smile would vanish, then she would start moving towards Krishna with a lurching gait that betrayed her alarm, only to stop short abruptly when the person turned and she saw it was an acquaintance who had come to greet the little hero. Her face would relax but the creases would remain. Nanda knew exactly how she felt because he felt the same way.

He prayed daily that the anxiety be removed from their lives. In a way, the warrior spirit within him wished that the assassins would show themselves sooner rather than later, so that this ordeal could end once and for all. It was the waiting and anticipation that caused the greatest distress.

six

When Kamsa felt he was somewhat calmer and ready for conversation, he sent for Pralamba. The old minister arrived, visibly nervous. He had probably got wind of the rumours about Kamsa's unusual mood following the news of Putana's death. The old man had been sidelined by Bahuka, Jarasandha's emissary who had been sent to oversee Kamsa during his most manic period following the birth and escape of the Slayer. Kamsa had been truly out of control then and, in retrospect, Pralamba knew that had Jarasandha not stepped in and taken measures to bolster up his regency, Mathura would have burned in a brutal civil war that would have left Kamsa without a kingdom to govern and the Yadavas without a king to oppress them. The unknown drug that Bahuka mixed in Kamsa's food, and perhaps even drink, had been effective, perhaps too effective. Not only had Kamsa lost his powers, including his ability to enlarge himself to gargantuan size with all the resultant side-effects – suppurating living growths sprouting from his festering skin being the most horrendous one – but he had also lost large chunks of time. He would sleep one night in spring and wake on a summer morning. During the interim, he would apparently be walking, talking, eating, drinking, living, breathing as usual, but in fact that was only a drug-induced walking coma. He had no recollection of the lost chunks of time, but during those fugue periods, he would be as docile and amiable as a puppet on a string attached to Bahuka's meaty fingers. And how the emissary had made Kamsa dance to his tunes! He had thrown open the coffers of the palace and given away the bulk of Kamsa's dynastic fortune, gathered over generations, to the people, using greed and the inevitable lusts and self-indulgence money brought, to lull the people into a false sense of security. By the time Jarasandha came to Mathura to cleverly claim allegiance of the Yadava nations to his Magadhan Empire, Kamsa could do little more than watch as his father-in-law ruled in his name.

It had taken Kamsa months to regain his self-confidence and strength, and after a violent encounter with Jarasandha's personal bodyguards – when he maimed and brutalized with ease four Mohini Fauj warriors in his own bedchamber, demonstrating his newfound strength and abilities – Jarasandha had been impressed. Kamsa had been cautious not to reveal more than was necessary, such as the fact that his powers were growing and increasing in intensity. What Jarasandha had seen was barely half of what he was capable of. Yet Putana had told him that he would take years still to come into his full powers and if he moved too soon, he would risk losing everything. It was one thing to smash the skulls of a few Mohinis, but quite another to go up against Jarasandha himself. Even Kamsa was not impetuous and impatient enough to do that just yet, perhaps he never would be. After all, Jarasandha was more useful as an ally than as an enemy. It was the knowledge that Jarasandha stood behind him that kept civil war from breaking out in his kingdom, and which forced tens of thousands of Yadavas to flee into exile rather than stay and fight openly. And it was the same knowledge that kept his neighbours from invading and attempting to take over Mathura.

But this was a different problem. This was the Slayer. An enemy who was not interested in regional politics or imperial ambitions. This was a being prophesied to destroy him. *Him. Kamsa!* Why? Because he had a great destiny, that was why. And all those born with a great destiny are bound to attract powerful enemies. Every great hero has a great villain. So Kamsa had his Slayer, an infant child born to his own sister under his own roof and who desired to murder his own uncle. If patricide was the word for the killing of one's father, and matricide for the murder of one's mother, what was murder of an uncle called? He did not know the word. He had disliked Sanskrit so intensely as a boy, he had tipped his Sanskrit guru out of a high tower window one morning after a particularly gruelling session on derivatives. But it was a crime nevertheless ... How could an infant, barely two years old, be a threat to him, Kamsa, the most powerful being in this part of the world? It was ludicrous. Yet that same infant had killed Putana, *his* Putana. And he would have to pay for that crime. Infant or no infant, Kamsa would put an end to it right there and then.

Pralamba stood before him as Kamsa paced the room, musing on his course of action. Finally, Kamsa turned and looked intently at the chief advisor. The older man blanched, his greying moustache twitching. Ever since Jarasandha's departure, he had lived in perpetual anxiety about his fate. Kamsa knew that other kings would have had the advisor put to the sword merely for fraternizing with the Magadhan emperor while he acted as de facto king of Mathura, but Jarasandha *was* Kamsa's father-in-law and Mathura *had* sworn allegiance to Magadha. So, strictly speaking, Pralamba had done no wrong. Even so, the man was never quite comfortable around his king, and Kamsa himself saw no reason to give the man reason to feel at ease.

True that Pralamba had not betrayed him entirely, but he had not demonstrated loyalty to Kamsa either. Had Kamsa not withstood the attack of the four Hijras in his own bedchamber and demolished those four unfortunates with crushing ease, they would have killed him and Pralamba would have stood by and watched. So would Pradyota, Putana's husband, for that matter, and for that reason Kamsa had a bone to pick with him as well. But this was not the rakshasa Kamsa they expected him to turn into, the festering giant who raged and rampaged at will, this was Kamsa the Terrible as he now liked to think of himself. A king so shrewd he had outwitted the great Jarasandha himself; and before his reign was over, would dethrone his father-in-law as well. And to achieve such great things, he needed every political support. Pralamba was an experienced advisor with keen knowledge of the Yadava tribes and clans and his spasa network was excellent. He was more useful to Kamsa alive than dead. And so long as he remained useful, he would stay alive.

Somehow, the advisor was canny enough to sense this and he seemed to grow visibly less anxious as Kamsa paced. After all, tyrants who lashed out viciously rarely took such a long time to brood over their actions beforehand. Even so, he was wise enough to gauge Kamsa's agitated state and to know better than to speak until spoken to; that was one of the reasons Kamsa had kept him around after Bahuka's departure – because of his canny judgement.

Finally, Kamsa turned to him. With offhand casualness he said, 'Gokuldham.'

Pralamba dipped his head to acknowledge that he had heard. 'What of it, your highness?'

'Burn it to the ground. Punishment for the murder of Putana, the wife of the captain of our guard. As a member of the royal staff, her heinous murder cannot go unpunished. Raze the entire settlement to the ground. Kill everyone living there. Also kill those who stand in the way or express sympathy for the dying.'

Pralamba was silent for longer than required. He did not object vocally, nor make any sound or gesture to indicate he disagreed with Kamsa's orders, nor did he give a simple and assertive 'yes, sire,' and leave to execute his king's orders. This was his diplomatic way of communicating to Kamsa that he disagreed but that it was up to Kamsa to ask him why he disagreed. Again, another excellent reason why he remained alive when virtually every last minister, advisor, preceptor and officer of the court had been executed or imprisoned in the past decade.

'Well?' Kamsa asked, his voice echoing in the empty throne chamber. 'Since you have not left to do my bidding I can only presume you wish to offer some objection. Speak!'

'Not an objection, your highness. Merely ... a doubt.'

Kamsa gestured impatiently, indicating to him to go on.

Pralamba went on with a mite more confidence, careful to keep his voice low and his gaze unchallenging.

'My lord, Gokuldham is governed by Nanda Maharaja.'

'So?'

'Nanda himself is a peaceful man. But he is dearly loved and supported by the people, particularly the Vrishni clan.'

Kamsa nodded grimly. 'And the Vrishnis are leaders of the rebellion. All the more reason to teach them a lesson.'

'True, my lord. The rebels must be dealt with firmly. But you propose to attack Gokuldham and harm Nanda and his people. They are peaceable folk and not directly involved in the rebellion.'

'They support, encourage, supply the rebels. Otherwise, Akrur and the other chieftains would not be able to sustain themselves for so long and harry our army this effectively,' Kamsa said. 'Ever since Vasudeva and Devaki scurried away like cowards ...' He clenched his fist in anger. The thought of his sister and her husband eluding his grasp still rankled; even though ostensibly they had left on a pilgrimage, his spasas informed him that their departure had given credibility and strength to the growing rebellion within his nation. Akrur, son of Svaphalka, was reportedly leading the rebellion with the Vrishnis at the fore of the Sura insurrection. Until now, they had only succeeded in harassing his army and defying his authority using symbolic actions rather than meaningful military tactics but any such defiance was a thorny barb in his flesh and could not be tolerated.'Gokuldham is the heart of Vrishni territory. It is not possible that this Nanda Maharaja and his people do not supply and provide the rebels with their needs. Punishing them will send a message to the rebels and curb the menace before it grows into a full-blown insurrection.'

Pralamba nodded slowly, unable to ignore the unshakeable logic of this argument.'What you say is true, sire. But attacking a peaceful hamlet such as Gokuldham and a revered community leader such as Nanda Maharaja will also send out a different message, one that you may not wish to send.'

Kamsa frowned.'What do you mean?'

'If we attack Gokul, not just the Vrishnis but all Sura Yadavas will rise against you. No Yadava can bear the slaughter of innocent gopas and gopis in the heartland.'

Kamsa shrugged. 'They are already harrying us through forays and petty insubordinations.'

'But this would be an all-out rebellion. They would raise up militia against you, with Akrur's Vrishnis leading the fray. We are not talking about a harmless assault or harassment.'

Kamsa was still not impressed. 'We Andhakas have fought the Suras for decades and are willing to continue if need be.'

Pralamba clearly wished to argue the point but he took a moment to pause and gather his wits before continuing. 'But if they rise this time, Drupad would support them. He might even join his forces with theirs.'

'Drupad? King of Panchal?' Kamsa snorted. 'Why would he risk making an enemy of Mathura?'

'Because he is already involved, sire. It is well known that he is sheltering tens of thousands of refugee Sura Yadavas who have fled to Panchal. And as you know full well, he has always coveted Mathura.'

Kamsa could not disagree. 'That he has,' he admitted reluctantly.

'And if Drupad joins the Sura Yadavas, Kuntibhoja will join in as well.'

Kamsa raised his head, thinking. 'Kuntibhoja regards Vasudeva's sister Pritha as his own daughter.'

'Indeed, sire, she is even known as Kunti for that reason.' Pralamba was wise enough to see that his liege had caught the thread of the argument and did not need to be prompted further. He waited as Kamsa rose from his throne and paced a few moments, thinking.

'And Kunti alias Pritha, Vasudeva's sister, is married to that discoloured king of Hastinapura, what's his name? White-face?'

'Pandurang,' Pralamba said.

'Yes, Pandu. So if Kuntibhoja joins in, there's a possibility of old man Bhishma putting Hastinapura's akshohinis into the alliance as well.' Kamsa walked over to a painted map depicting the Bharata subcontinent. He considered the forces that would be aligned against him, jabbing his finger against the heavy canvas as he called out each name: 'The Suras. Panchala. Bhoja. Hastinapura.'

Eyes glittering, he turned to look down at Pralamba. 'Is it a coincidence that all these happen to be territories that have successfully resisted the efforts of Jarasandha and remain hostile to the empire of Magadha?'

'Nay, sire. It is no coincidence. That is another reason why they are waiting only for an excuse to open a war front with Mathura. They regard Mathura as a weak—' The old advisor bit off his words in mid-sentence. He was about to say 'weak link' but had just realized how that might sound to the ruler of that alleged 'weak' link. 'As a possible bargaining tool,' he continued, 'and hope that by fighting and crushing Mathura they will force Jarasandha to break off his campaign against the other territories and return here to defend you, his son-in-law, as well as Mathura, the pride of his empire. Tactically, that would make it impossible for Jarasandha to continue his campaign of expansion and consolidation. If Jarasandha has to stay and defend Mathura on so many fronts—' The advisor gestured at the map which depicted Mathura surrounded by the territories Kamsa had just pointed out. 'It would effectively bring the Magadhan campaign to a grinding halt. Through shrewd alliances with the other nations, they would throw Jarasandha's forces out from there as well, and push him back to the western frontier provinces, leaving him nowhere to go except the far western mlechcha lands.'

Pralamba was an old horse and when he referred to the far western lands as 'mlechcha', he put every nuance of derogatory inflection into that term. To the old guard, those regions west of the Kusa ranges were not merely barbaric and uncivilized, they were undesirable.

Kamsa thought about this for several moments. He could not find any reason to disagree with anything Pralamba had said. Yet he seethed at the thought of letting Putana's death go unavenged.

He dismissed Pralamba abruptly and sat brooding.

Somehow, he had to find a way to get at that brat and destroy him once and for all. It was no longer a question of his own survival. It was revenge, pure and simple. In the meantime, he reassured himself reluctantly, three assassins still remained to do their job. He could at least hope they would fare better than Putana.

seven

As the days passed and Krishna still did not speak to her as he had before, Yashoda began to wonder if the attack had affected him somehow. They had ascertained that Putana had been attempting to feed him poisoned milk. That he had survived was a miracle due partly to his own extraordinary nature, she knew, but what if the poison had affected him in some way. The deep sleep he had fallen into immediately following the incident, the fact that he hadn't spoken to her mind as he used to so frequently before, troubled her. At the same time, he seemed quite normal and playful; his appetite was as healthy as ever, and when watching him at play with his brother Balarama, everything seemed quite normal. But that was the point: her Krishna was not quite normal, he was more than that. As days went by and he seemed like all the other infants his age – sons and daughters of her sisters and friends who came daily to play with him and Balarama – she began to doubt her own memory. Had she actually heard him speak to her within her mind? Could it have been motherly instinct that made her certain she knew what he was thinking? What about the cart he had shattered with a single kick of his little foot? Had that truly been the work of some rakshasa and had it been Vishnu's divine hand that had spared him rather than his own supernormal abilities?

She hesitated to bring up these matters with Nanda – he seemed preoccupied and distracted as well. There was talk of rebellion and of an alliance against Mathura. Nanda had always been clear on the matter of politics: whatever the problem, war and violence could never be solutions to anything. His staunch insistence on pacificism was a necessary counterpoint to the constant heated tempers and enraged debates, though it frustrated those who felt that the time for talk and peaceful methods was long past. Vasudeva and Devaki had escaped into exile and nobody knew exactly where they were even now, only that they were safe and well. She was relieved about that. She was less relieved to hear that Akrur and the Vrishni rebels had bartered an alliance with Drupad, king of Panchal. She did not know much about politics, but Nanda spoke to her when his mind overflowed with worries and he felt that Drupad was an ambitious and grasping king, a warmonger who would rouse his army and ride on Mathura without much provocation. He felt that Akrur had erred in bringing him into the fray. But Panchal was the only nation willing to shelter the fleeing Sura refugees seeking to escape the Usurper's yoke and risk incurring the wrath of Kamsa, and such support came at a heavy price.

If Akrur reached an agreement with Drupad, Panchal would march on Mathura. And if Panchal's army attacked Mathura, Bhoja could not stay neutral. King Kuntibhoja would have to join them, if only because, as adoptive father of Vasudeva's sister Pritha alias Kunti, he was obliged to do so. And if Kunti's adoptive father joined in, her husband Pandu might be similarly motivated. Pandu himself did not have sufficient power to commit Hastinapura's considerable might but his pitamah, Bhishma of the Terrible Vow, certainly did. And if Bhishma Pitamah aligned with the forces against Mathura, it was almost certain that Jarasandha the Magadhan would join in the melee. It would be a war on every front and it could be decades, or even centuries, before peace descended on the Yadavas again. Nanda knew and feared this more than the actual threat of violence. It was one thing to suffer the yoke of Kamsa, but was it worth risking a century of war to overthrow that yoke? And who was to say what the eventual outcome might be? After all, the Bharata dynasty – from which Hastinapura's rulers were descended, specifically the Puru line – was the forebear of the Yadavas. And Yadu had been made an outcast by his own father Yayati, banished to these regions. There were still tribes who recalled that ancient humiliation and resented it, believing that Yadavas had equal claim to the throne of the City of Elephants, Hastinapura, or as they preferred to call it with deliberate irony, Nagapura, City of Snakes. What might begin as a sincere attempt to support an oppressed people and overthrow a tyrant usurper might well end up as a war engulfing the entire subcontinent. War was like a half-starved, wound-maddened tiger unleashed in a closed house full of people: the only certain outcome was that people would die. Who and why did not matter to the tiger of war.

So Yashoda kept silent about her concerns, thinking she would give it another day or two, then another week, then another fortnight. And as the weeks passed, she began to resign herself to the change in her beloved Krishna. So what if he could not speak to her through her mind any longer? He was still her beloved one. He was healthy, happy, playful ... most of all, he was alive! She was grateful for that.

Now that Krishna was walking, it was harder to keep track of him. Most infants took a few steps one day, then stumbled and fell, then gradually progressed over the next few weeks. Not

Krishna. One day he was sitting and creeping and crawling, the next he was dancing on Putana's corpse, and from that day onwards, he walked like any toddler. He lurched, he stumbled, he almost fell – and sometimes actually fell – but mostly he regained his balance and continued on his merry way. He had some trouble going downhill. On one occasion, Krishna was sitting beside Yashoda and playing with a wooden wagon cart. Yashoda heard her name called by Aindavi and Kirtida, her best friends, and turned her head for a moment. As they approached, Aindavi put her hand to her mouth and screamed. She pointed over Yashoda's shoulder and, her heart leaping with panic, Yashoda turned and saw Krishna trundling down the grassy slope. The cart had got away from him and was rolling downhill and he had risen to follow it. The cart picked up speed as it rolled and so did Krishna, his chubby arms raised and waving as he sought to maintain his balance. The pull of Prithvi Maa drew him down and he ran faster after the rolling toy cart. Yashoda called his name and ran after him, followed closely by her friends. She could hear Krishna laughing in his baby gurgle as he went, and it was evident that he was neither afraid nor aware of the possibility of coming to harm.

About halfway downhill, he lost his balance, and went head over heels on the grass – and kept going. Yashoda gasped, running faster. Krishna tumbled a few times, then came to a rest, sitting up. His heavy head jerked forward on his slight neck and he released a choked burst of laughter. Yashoda came running up beside him and crouched down, cradling him to her chest, swaying from side to side, tears of relief pouring down her face. Her friends bent beside her, reassuring her, touching her arms, touching Krishna, and she realized in that moment that divine or mortal, it didn't matter to a mother's heart. To a mother, even a god infant was still her son and even if he was invulnerable to every conceivable danger, she would still worry her heart out over him.

When she finally released Krishna from her smothering embrace, he smiled up at her proudly and held up his fist.

'Maa!' he cried, the only word he could speak aloud. The wooden cart was clutched in his chubby fist.

'Maa!' he cried again, waving the cart at her until she nodded and acknowledged his triumph.

He had chased down the cart and caught it. To him, it had been a little adventure, nothing more. Soon after, he had his milk, burped happily, then fell asleep with arms and legs sprawled as usual, the wooden cart still clutched in his fist. Yashoda tried to prise it loose but when the wood creaked as if it was about to crack, she let go at once. Her child wasn't about to give up his prize that easily.

After that first little triumph, the adventures increased in number.

One day she was feeding one of the cows, Krishna beside her. He loved being around the cows. He had a way of putting his hand on their bellies, palm pressed upwards so he could reach their bulging stomachs, and making a resonant nasal sound in his sinus before saying, 'Maa!' It was possible he meant to say something completely different but, at the moment, that was the only word he could utter. As it happened, it was an appropriate term to use: cows were quite literally gou-mata. Cow-mothers. Yashoda couldn't help feeling that even Krishna's little ritual of placing his palm on their bellies and making that odd sound was a kind of blessing.

She wasn't in the least surprised when the cows began yielding richer, sweeter milk than ever before. She was quite certain they were the very cows her little Krishna had touched … though perhaps *blessed* was the right word.

There came a day when she came out of her front door to find every untethered cow gathered outside, waiting patiently. She stopped short, taken aback. The cows stood silently, as if waiting for something or someone. Moments later, the pitter-patter of little bare feet sounded and her dark rascal came to the threshold. At once, the cows sent up such a lowing and mooing that people came rushing from around the house to see what was going on. Krishna clapped his hands gleefully, smacking the palms together in that uncoordinated way infants have, sometimes missing and slapping empty air, giggling open-mouthed. Then he raised both his palms and showed them to the gathering of cows. They subsided at once. One solitary calf right at the back, probably unable to see from behind the big cows, lowed once, plaintively. Krishna put his finger to his lips and said, 'Shhh!' The calf subsided as well.

Then, as Yashoda and the other family members watched in amazement, he began making that nasal sound again. Except that this time, despite his inability to pronounce words clearly just yet, it was almost recognizable. Yashoda felt certain that it was the sacred syllable Om. But the way Krishna made the sound, it was deeper, more primal somehow, like something that transcended language and words and meaning. Something that went back to the beginning of time and the human race. It was a sound filled with great power and history, made by the nasal septum of a two-year-old infant standing naked on his doorstep!

Then he raised his palm again and held it out to the gathered cows. Yashoda blinked as something passed from that open palm to the cows. She couldn't say what it was exactly. It was not light, not quite a glow. It was wholly invisible. Nothing actually was seen coming from his open palm. Yet something did emanate from him and pass to the cows. Something that she could only describe as … a force. An energy. A blessing.

The cows lowed loudly again, this time with a tone of satisfaction, the sad-sack tone of cows since time immemorial, then turned ponderously and clumped their way back to their foraging grounds and tabelas. They didn't need to be herded; they found their way quite well by themselves.

Only the little calf remained. Hanging back, he began to follow his mother, then hesitated and turned his head back, looking mournfully at Krishna.

Krishna smiled. Yashoda saw him beaming brightly as if he knew exactly what ailed the little calf. And he stepped off the threshold, almost losing his balance in the process, onto the soft grassy ground of the courtyard. She felt her arms reach out instinctively to grab him, but saw that he needed no help. He padded across the courtyard to where the calf stood, waiting uncertainly.

He laughed and threw his little arms up to the calf's neck. It was still much too wide for him to embrace. But he somehow seemed to be able to enclose it in his arms and to everyone's surprise he gave it a big wet kiss on its lips. The calf lowed softly in surprise, then fell quiet. Krishna laughed and swung onto the calf's back, sitting astride it as he must have seen some of his fellow young gopas and gopis do.

The calf seemed pleased and lurched forward, running after its mother, following the herd. Krishna held on easily, laughing his gurgling laugh, absolutely fearless. Seeing him heading downhill, the gopas and gopis closest to him began to shout out warnings and run after him. Krishna continued undaunted, squealing with joy. The calf mirrored his childish enthusiasm, galloping like a horse.

'Maa!' cried Krishna happily as he passed over the hilltop and out of sight. 'Maa!'

It was still the only word he could speak aloud.

Shaking her head in amused despair, Yashoda ran after him. Even though she knew no harm would come to him, she could not simply stand there as her son rode recklessly down the hillside.

From that day onwards to the end of its days, that little calf never once fell ill or had any complaints or problems. Eventually, it would outlive every cow in the land. It was only much, much later that people realized the connection and harked back to the day Krishna had blessed it with his own life-essence, shared through a kiss.

eight

Kamsa threw aside his quilts and rose from his bed. Moonlight streamed in through his open windows, casting long shadows on the marbled floor. Unable to go back to sleep, unable to decide what to do with himself, he paced the floor for several moments. He had not slept well a single night since the news of Putana's death. His position made it impossible for him to unburden his mind to anyone at court. There were the concubines but he had never trusted any of them even as a boy; he was hardly able to trust them now. He had issues when it came to trust. And when his own sister had betrayed him by marrying their worst enemy and had then birthed the child who would grow up to slay him, it was only natural.

He missed the time he had spent with Jarasandha, riding and fighting, and with barely time to recover one's energies and nurse one's wounds. Being under the command of a powerful leader, one who knew what he was doing and how to command, he had been able to absolve himself of all worry. He had lived moment by moment, fight by fight, battle by battle. He had survived some close encounters, each one feeling like a major victory. He had slaughtered many enemies, and each death had strengthened him. He was a warrior. Fighting was what he did best. Even leading men on a battlefield was not as satisfying: one always had to think of tactics and strategy and counter-

attack and defence and retreat and supply chains and all the
paraphernalia that went with commanding armies. As a warrior,
he could simply fight and kill, and move on without a second
thought or backward glance. The earth had been his to roam,
its every treasure his to take, and all problems could be solved
with the blade of a sword.

He longed for that simple life again: to take up his sword
and venture forth; to rejoin Jarasandha and ride out with his
forces; to fight mindlessly, knowing only the relentless intensity
of warcraft and bloodshed, survival and slaughter. No thought
of tomorrow, no cares beyond surviving the present moment,
no time to worry. But things had changed between him and the
Magadhan. For one thing, Jarasandha was his father-in-law,
and Kamsa's two lovely wives awaited his return in their idyllic
palace, awaited his return so that he might do his conjugal duty
and seed them both with child. And much as he desired those
two wonderful women, and would want nothing more than to
plough their fertile fields and seed them, the fact that Jarasandha
wanted it made him reluctant. To Jarasandha, everything was
politics and power. He had given his daughters in marriage to
Kamsa in order to tie his own bloodline to that of the Yadavas. It
was that tie that had given him the right to march into Mathura
not long ago and assume regency of the kingdom during the
period of Kamsa's apparent 'illness'. That the 'illness' in question
was nothing more than the work of Jarasandha's own spasa
Bahuka – planted in Kamsa's palace by the Magadhan – and
caused by the mixing of an unknown potion in Kamsa's food
or drink over several months were not known to anyone but
Kamsa. The results of the poisoning, if it could be called that,
were for everyone to see as they were striking: from a powerful
rakshasa capable of expanding himself to a height of several

hundred feet if he desired, Kamsa was reduced to a mindless husk of a mortal man – one who was barely able to keep track of what day it was and what had happened the day before, or what he had eaten for his morning meal that same day. His rakshasa powers had been taken from him in one cruel swipe. Then again, as he had discovered recently, it was Jarasandha himself who had fed him certain potions that had caused that very rakshasa nature to surface in the first place. So, looking back now as he paced his chamber by moonlight, Kamsa realized how obvious the whole plan had been: Jarasandha had intended all along to awaken Kamsa's rakshasa nature so that he would overthrow his father and usurp the throne, then, when that very rakshasa powers caused Kamsa to lose control and go on a rampage of bloodshed that threatened to make his own people rise against him, Jarasandha had countered the first potion's effect with a second one, altering Kamsa's physiology yet again.

However, unknown to the Magadhan, Putana had come to Kamsa's aid, her toxic milk enabling Kamsa to increase his density while outwardly retaining the same size and form. Kamsa had enhanced this new ability to the point where he was the equal of any of Jarasandha's own supernaturally empowered champions. Impressed by his son-in-law's newfound abilities and the apparent maturity that came with the change, Jarasandha had withdrawn his forces from Mathura, with the understanding that Kamsa would abide by their alliance and father heirs upon both his daughters at the earliest.

Now, the day of reckoning was approaching soon. With Putana's plan to assassinate the Slayer before he grew to full strength having failed, Kamsa seemed to be left with no real options. Only that morning he had received a missive from Jarasandha, summoning him to a conference of kings. The

Magadhan's empire had grown to a formidable extent: not as large as Jarasandha himself had envisaged and desired as yet, but far greater than what any other kingdom in Aryavarta had expected only a few short years ago. There was no question of opposing Jarasandha, not with the Yadavas themselves in revolt against their ruler. And as Pralamba had wisely reminded him, there were a number of other neighbouring kingdoms with their own political ambitions and agendas. The instant he weakened or took a misstep, Kamsa reckoned, Mathura would be wrested from him as easily as a battlefield crow snatches away a morsel of flesh. He could not afford to make a mistake.

This was the only reason he still suffered the Slayer to live.

Weary of pacing the same floors he left his chambers and strode out into the moonlit night. He headed for the stables, not because he wished to ride but because he did not know what else to do. He needed to do something that would distract him from his political anxieties. Something that involved pulverizing boulders or smashing skulls would be wonderful.

The stable house was dark, silent and redolent of horse droppings. Kamsa walked the length, trying to decide which horse would be strong enough to put up a decent fight. The animals were asleep but at his scent, they woke up and began to whicker softly to one another. At least a few bared their teeth in the darkness, threatening to nip at him if he came within reach. Amused, he held out a finger to one, a mean-spirited grey beast that was the get of a horse imported from the Arabi deserts during his father's reign. The stallion snapped hard at his finger, hard enough to bite off any man's finger clean through the bone. But Kamsa was not any man; he had hardened his density just enough to test the horse's bite. The beast's powerful jaw clamped down on a finger that was denser than the hardest oak, not quite as solid as iron. Kamsa heard the sound of bone chipping and felt the horse's tooth crack. The stallion's eyes widened in shock and he reared back. Never before had he bitten any living being capable of withstanding his powerful jaws. Kamsa had a feeling he would never bite anyone again either. He laughed and moved on to the next.

'Why harry the horses? Surely you are man enough to face a more wily opponent?'

The voice was quiet, challenging, even mocking. It came from the darkness at the far end of the stable house, from the shadows where the moonlight streaming through the open doors did not reach. Kamsa squinted but his extraordinary abilities did not include the power to see in the dark. The stench of fresh horse manure came to him strongly; the Arabi stallion had vented his bowels in shock and several others, sensing their fellow's distress, had followed suit.

'Who's there?' Kamsa said in a normal voice. He had no need to raise his voice or to insert any inflection. He was king of the realm and was possessed of powers no mortal foe could withstand. Fear was not part of his mental composition. But he was genuinely curious. Who would be at the stable at this unearthly hour? And what man would dare address him thus? For a moment, he thought of Pradyota. The captain of his guard had been devastated by the news of the death of his wife – allegedly killed in an accident while on a routine visit to Vraj – but as far as Kamsa knew, he had no idea of Kamsa's 'special' relationship with Putana, nor the real reason why she had gone visiting Vraj. Putana had been very astute in keeping her true nature a secret from her mortal husband; she had been keeping that secret for a very, very long time from a great many husbands. Still, Kamsa constantly felt a twinge of unfamiliar emotion every time Pradyota came to him for official matters. He was even tempted to unburden his heart to the man, to share their mutual grief at the loss of the woman whose love they had both shared, albeit in very different ways. Kamsa had not been a husband to Putana in the sense that Pradyota had, yet he had shared a bond with her that was more intimate and secret than that between husband and wife. He doubted Pradyota would understand and, in any case, he had no intention of letting out Putana's secret. What would the point be, now that she was dead? So he had kept his mouth shut and his emotions bottled but now, in this darkened stable house, for some reason he thought perhaps, just perhaps, the man addressing him might be the captain.

The dark figure separated from the shadows at the far wall and approached Kamsa. As he came closer, the moonlight was still insufficient to illuminate him fully. But at least Kamsa could make out who he was. It was not Pradyota, he realized, and felt an irrational rush of relief at the knowledge.

It was the old stablehand, the ancient fellow who had always been around for as long as Kamsa could remember. He had been the one who brought the pony on which Kamsa took his first ride, and even then he had looked ancient. Kamsa rarely bothered with menial help, but the man's constancy in the ever-shifting firmament of his life was unusual enough for him to have glanced occasionally at the worn parchment map of the old syce's face – creased with a thousand wrinkles – and wondered how anyone could live that long. Kamsa's interest quickened when he remembered what Narada-muni had told him in that last cryptic communication: that Yadu would aid him in his quest. This old bag of bones? Impossible! Yet there was something about the old syce that made Kamsa uneasy, as uneasy as he had felt when he had been but a boy and his father Ugrasena had been in his prime, a roaring, hard-drinking, battle-mongering lion of a man, back when Kamsa had actually feared him. For some reason, he felt a prickle of that same fear when the old syce looked at him through those ancient eyes.

Come to think of it, the old man had also been there while Putana and Kamsa had worked on developing Kamsa's newfound abilities. He might not have been present when they went out into the wilderness to execute the more elaborate training regimes Putana had put him through, but he had seen enough to know that the king's new strength was unusual. Kamsa had wondered aloud if he could be trusted and Putana had glanced back at the old man and smiled an odd smile before replying in the positive. Kamsa remembered that odd smile now and wondered what it had meant.

In the darkness, with barely enough light to reveal the outline of the old man's form, the thousand wrinkles were not visible, nor were the other signs of age and decrepitude. He was just a man-shaped being standing in the shadows, no distinctive features or details visible. He could be anyone, any age, any race. And when he spoke again, his voice did not betray his age either. This lent him an air of menace that Kamsa had never sensed in him before. Perhaps it was just the way he stood in the shadows, legs akimbo, arms dangling loosely by his side, eyes glinting in the shadows as he stared directly at his king, undaunted by his knowledge of Kamsa's true abilities and of his royalty.

'What did you say, old man?' Kamsa asked softly. He was spoiling for a fight and while there was no real challenge in taking on an old man, if this was all that was available, he would not refuse it. Horses, rhinoceros, men … a skull was a skull, and smashing one was all he desired right then.

The old stablehand said nothing for a moment. Kamsa assumed that the man had realized his mistake and was recalcitrant now. Not that it would save him. He was due a punishment. But then the syce spoke again and this time there was no mistaking the raw menace and challenge in his voice. Even Kamsa was a little surprised at the gruff arrogance in the man's words. It was one thing to make a remark in passing and quite another to retort to a man's face, particularly when that man was King Kamsa, the Marauder of Mathura.

'You grieve for your lost woman, yet all she did was lie and deceive you to the very end. You thought she helped you because she wished you to succeed in killing your prophesied slayer. But all she truly desired was her own moksha.'

What was the old man blabbering about? 'Are you speaking of Lady Putana?' Kamsa asked. He was so surprised at the man's words, he forgot his anger for a moment. Of all the nonsense he had thought the old man might spout, speaking of Putana so intimately had not been anticipated. 'What do you know about her, you muck-raker?'

The old man shifted slightly, or perhaps it was the moonlight that moved behind Kamsa, illuminating the ancient wizened face a little more. He could see more than just the man's eyes now. It almost appeared as if the creases and lines on that ancient face had smoothened and he was as young and robust as he had been when he was as young as Kamsa himself. *A trick of the light and shadows, nothing more*, Kamsa thought.

'I know more than you ever will,' said the oldun. 'I know that she sought to die at the hands of the Slayer, because to be killed by the Eighth Child guarantees direct ascension to the heavenly realms. That was the only reason why she played along with your puerile games and pathetic attempts at thwarting the inevitable.'

Kamsa's eyes widened. 'What did you just say?' He clenched his fists and took a step forward, feeling his flesh harden instantly. 'How dare you, insolent old fool!'

'Silence!' barked the stablehand. 'You may not have been taught to respect your elders but you will show me respect when I speak to you, boy. I may rake the muck your horses make and work all day in these stinking stables, but I am still your elder and you will show my age the respect it deserves.'

Kamsa was astonished. Did the man wish to die right there and then? Clearly, he was out of his senses, senile probably.

'Who do you think you are? Don't you know whom you speak to? I am—'

He got no further. The old man was on him before Kamsa could speak his own name out loud. Kamsa felt a powerful hand upon his throat, clutching his Adam's apple in a grip of steel, and the old man's breath on his cheek. It reeked of old apples and saffron. The man himself stank of horse shit and sweat. But it was the hand on his throat that had Kamsa's attention: he had hardened his body to the consistency of iron layered several dozen times, hard enough for a sword swung with full force at even the softest part of his body to shatter to shards without nicking him. Yet the old man had grasped his throat in a grip that could crush him instantly. Kamsa felt the force of that grip, felt the pain in his Adam's apple, like something lodged in his throat, and knew that despite his great invulnerability and ability, the old syce was stronger and more powerful and could kill him on the spot if he desired.

'I know exactly who you are,' said the old man, a faint spray of spittle coating Kamsa's face as he hissed the words from an inch away. 'You are the guttersnipe who overthrew one of the greatest kings that ruled Mathura and usurped the Yadava throne, plunging this great nation into the darkest age of its history. I should rip your throat out and let you bleed on this manure-stained floor while the horses snicker, for I cannot brook letting you sit upon my throne for a day longer and destroy all that I spent my life building. I have seen you do too much damage to this great nation already, I cannot watch any longer. Say one wrong word and I shall kill you where you stand.'

nine

'Yashoda, come on! You'll miss the start!' cried her friends. Her sisters were out of sight, probably joining in the festivities already. Not for the first time she wished Nanda was with her. But as host of the event, he had to go ahead to ensure that all was in order for the ras-lila. Normally, she would have taken care of all the arrangements: she loved the process of selecting flowers for the garlands, supervising the decorations, the setting up of the tents and stalls, the preparation of the food, the whole noise and bustle and rushing madness of the whole event. She thrived on being in charge and putting together elaborate arrangements for feasts and festivities at short notice. Nanda had even asked her tentatively if she wished to involve herself, either wholly or partially, but it was she who had refused. She knew how hectic such things got and once she had dipped her toe in the water, she would not be able to resist diving in, so to speak. And in all that hustle and bustle and giving of orders and supervising a hundred different things at the same time, she could not possibly keep a constant watch on Krishna.

And she could not accept anything less.

Krishna was all that mattered to her now. She would not have anything happening to him on her account. Nanda's burly fellows with their lathis could watch over him and twirl their oiled moustaches all day and night, but only a mother's eyes really could keep track of a little tyke. As anyone who has ever raised a child knows full well, sooner or later there comes a moment when one looks away, or turns one's head, or lifts one's eyes for a moment, just a moment, and somehow, through the peculiar powers unique to their ilk, infants find a way to put themselves in harm's way precisely in that instant. For her to involve herself in the ras-lila arrangements would mean entrusting his safety to the watchmen. She could not do that. Not yet. Perhaps not ever.

So there she was, among the last to arrive at her own festivities, rushing to keep up with the others. She was all dressed and bejewelled and was pleased that she had only grown slightly plumper than before she had birthed Krishna. Not that Nanda minded, for plumpness ran in her family and he favoured her being 'healthy' rather than lean – as he had told her on many an occasion, making her blush. She wanted to fit into the same ras suit she had worn before her pregnancy, her favourite green and yellow and purple one, and she did. With just a little adjustment at the seams, but not much. She looked forward to an afternoon with her friends and sisters and their families, dancing and clicking sticks and singing the ritual songs together. She could do with a little laughter and cheer.

'Yashoda!' her friends cried, disappearing over the top of the hill. She saw them crying out with delight as they looked down at the festival grounds on the far side of the hill, then disappear from sight. She wished she could simply run up the sloping rise and down the other side, as she and her sakhis had done when they were children. But it was a good three hundred yards uphill in a gentle gradient, with hummocks and rabbit holes everywhere and she was already out of breath. My, but if she hadn't put on weight, why did she feel so heavy?

'Maa,' Krishna gurgled sleepily. He had just drunk a stomachful of milk before they left. As if acknowledging the fact, he burped now, loud and long, the sound almost making her giggle out loud. 'Maa,' he said again, contended, then his head lolled on her shoulder. She staggered back, almost losing her footing entirely and tumbling backwards.

She glanced around. The bodyguards were behind her, about ten or fifteen yards away, talking genially with one another. They were supposed to maintain a cordon around her at all times, but as the days passed they had grown bored of standing alone out of talking distance and had taken to strolling in pairs, chatting incessantly. The two closest to her were aware of her but not looking directly at her. In any case, if she did actually tumble over, they were too far to reach her in time.

She took another step uphill and gasped. Great goddess! Who said she hadn't become fat? She felt absolutely humongous right now. As if she had put on a hundred-kilo weight. Or a thousand!

Another step, and this time she could actually feel her bones creaking with the strain. This was ridiculous. She could barely move. She stopped and leaned against a tree. Sweat stains were spreading around her underarms and down her back. She was exhausted even before she reached the ras-lila! How was she going to dance?

Krishna's head lolled a little and somehow his momentum carried his head down her shoulder. The side of his head touched the trunk lightly, just a feather brush.

The bark of the tree split apart.

It cracked and fell in powdery fragments.

Yashoda frowned and looked closely at the tree trunk, at the spot where Krishna's head had touched it.

The trunk had cracked.

There was a distinct line running through it.

She blinked, bewildered.

What did that mean?

She glanced at Krishna who was fast asleep. Then she looked down at the arm holding him and tried to adjust it a little for comfort. The arm screamed with agony. She realized that the muscles she thought had stiffened had actually been strained to the point where they could take no more weight. They cried in protest as she tried to shift Krishna to her other hand.

Sweat pouring down her face and neck, staining the blouse of her best ras-lila suit, she struggled to lower Krishna to the ground. Somehow, with a mighty effort, she managed to place him on the ground at the foot of the sala tree. She rested his head and back against the trunk of the tree. His head rolled forward, then swung back instinctively, striking the trunk. It was just a nudge, really. Her Krishna was a tough boy that way, often competing with his half-brother Balarama in demonstrating how much he could bear without crying – although when it came down to push and shove, it was always Krishna who called 'Maa' before Balarama asked for Rohini.

The tree trunk split with a resounding crack.

She gasped and reared back. For an instant, she thought the tree itself was about to tip over. The cracking sound was followed by a groaning sound and the tree itself swayed and shook. Monkeys and birds resting on the branches above cried out and leapt away or took flight in alarm. Then, with a deep moan, the tree seemed to settle and held still.

Yashoda swallowed nervously, wiping the sweat from her face with a fold of her garment. Krishna lay back against the tree trunk, sound asleep, his lips pouting slightly as if they had just left off suckling.

She glanced around. The bodyguards were coming towards her, having heard the sound of the tree and the commotion of the wildlife. One raised a hand questioningly. She shook her head, indicating that nothing was wrong. And it was true: nothing was wrong. Yet something had just happened. What? She realized that she suddenly felt lighter, much lighter than when she had begun climbing the hill. She got back warily to her feet and yes, she was feeling so much lighter that she could have run up to the top of the hill and down the other side, as her friends had done. But how was that possible? What had changed?

Krishna stirred a little in his sleep, making that baby-snoring nasal sound he sometimes made, and the tree groaned again. A few more birds that had just begun to resettle took off again. A monkey screeched indignantly some distance away, complaining about the two-footed strangers who had come and disturbed the peace.

In a flash, Yashoda understood.

Krishna! She had been carrying him when she had begun feeling heavier. He had been falling asleep at the time and as he had gone deeper into sleep, he had grown heavier.

And when she put him down against the tree trunk, the tree had cracked at the touch of his head. Just now, when he had shifted, the tree had protested.

Somehow, her Krishna had increased in weight.

But how was that possible?

He was just a babe, asleep. Even if he was touched by divinity, what did that have to do with his weight?

The sound of a flute came to her from over the hill, followed an instant later by the sound of laughter and other music and the clacking of sticks. The ras-lila had begun.

She bent down and took hold of Krishna as she usually did, gripping him under the arms. He had grown too big for her to pick up with one arm around his back as she might have done a year ago, but now, even with both hands gripping him firmly and using all her strength, she could not budge him! She strained, using her back to exert force, the way she did when pulling a heavy object. Yashoda was not a delicate woman. Like any Vrishni Yadava, she had always done her share of the work, and cattle herding and dairy farming required strong hands and an even stronger back. Apart from that, she had always been athletic and good at games as a girl, especially games like kabaddi and lathi wielding. If anything, with a mother's workload and a baby to carry around everywhere, she had only grown stronger since then.

Yet, try as hard as she might, she could not make little Krishna budge. All she could manage was to lift his chubby little finger off his lap, and even that was as hard as lifting a heavy grinding stone!

She slumped back, staring in bewilderment at her little wonder. He remained sound asleep, leaning back against the trunk of the sala tree – which had bent at a noticeable angle by now but still sustained his weight – puckered mouth issuing a faint whistling sound every time he exhaled.

Something flashed inside his mouth.

Yashoda's heart leapt in her chest.

She leaned forward, watching closely. In the distance, the sound of the ras-lila increased in intensity, but her entire attention was focussed on her little beauty. He continued sleeping soundly but she was sure she had glimpsed something inside his little mouth.

There! She saw it again. Like a tiny light flashing.

There was something in his mouth. She was certain of it now.

Her heart pounded as she reached for her child's lips. They were already puckered, so she instinctively touched the tip of her little finger to the conjunction. He reacted at once and pushed his lips outward, then pulled them inward again. She withdrew her finger, and his lips parted at once, seeking the source of nourishment with the instinct of infants since the beginning of time. When he did not find it, his dark face crinkled in a disapproving frown.

Then he yawned.

His mouth opened wide, revealing his baby teeth and pink gums and the inside of his mouth and the passage of his throat.

Yashoda peered inside, trying to see what it was she had glimpsed, flashing or blinking.

She froze, staring.

Her breath paused in her throat.

Her entire being ceased.

She stumbled back, almost falling over, then caught her balance and rose to her feet. She stared down at her little baby, asleep against the sala tree, his mouth now closed, the yawn completed. Her palm was clasped across her mouth, covering it in the universal gesture of shock.

'Yashoda!'

Someone was calling her name.

She turned and looked uphill, and saw Nanda, silhouetted against the top of the hill, waving.

'Yashoda, come on! The ras-lila has started!'

She started towards Nanda, wanting to go to him, to tell him what she had just seen inside their little babe's mouth. What she had witnessed made her head reel. It was all she could do not to break into a run and sprint uphill to her husband, to fall into his arms, gasping and crying, and unburden her mind of the impossible sight that she had seen.

She took several steps uphill, her feet moving of their own accord. Then she realized that she could not simply leave Krishna lying there asleep under the sala tree – which was bent over at an alarming angle now, as if even in his sleep Krishna had pushed it back until the angle suited his comfort. The bodyguards were nearby, watching her in puzzlement, unable to understand what was alarming her so, yet realizing that something was amiss.

'Yashoda? Everything is well, no?' called Nanda from the top of the rise. He sensed something amiss as well.

Yashoda turned to call out to her husband, to beckon and ask him to come down so she could speak with him. She wanted to show him what she had just seen, to confirm that she had not simply imagined it, that it was real and not a product of her hysterical imagination.

But before she could call out or say a single word, a whirlwind struck.

ten

Kamsa was awakened by the sound of someone trying to break down the doors of his bedchamber. Raising a hand to shield his eyes from the gaudy sunlight streaming in through the uncurtained doors of the verandah, he staggered out of bed and unbolted the door. Four tall bald heads glared menacingly at him. Mohinis.

'The emperor wishes to see you at once.'

Kamsa blinked. 'Jarasandha? In Mathura?'

'No. We are to take you to him at once.'

The quad of eunuchs was in his bedchamber, watching and following as he moved around, trying to awaken his sleep-deprived mind. Water, he needed water right away. He had been up till early that morning. Even now, his body ached and protested with every move. That old syce! Of course, he reflected sombrely, he had not been merely an old syce at all. He had been something quite different. But he had no time to reflect on that now. The Hijras were hustling him with their customary aggressive efficiency.

'Must it be today itself?' he asked, already knowing the answer.

'His orders were to take you to him immediately,' one of them said. 'It is most of a day's journey. We must leave this very instant.'

Ever since his ability had manifested, Kamsa had taken to storing at least three large pots of water in his bedchamber, ensuring they were kept filled at all times. After a hard session working out in the wilderness, he was always stricken by a prodigious thirst. He would often awake at night with the same parched sensation.

One pot was half empty. He picked it up and drained the contents in a moment. When he lowered it and reached for the next, he noticed the Hijras watching with interest. He knew that they were impressed by his ability to lift the heavy pot with a single hand but also knew that they would never show it. When he had drained the first pot, he used his free hand to pick up the second one, which was so full that a little water sloshed over the side when he picked it up. He straightened it and raised it up as he lowered the first one. He saw the Mohinis' eyes cutting to one another. Now he knew that they were impressed by his ability to balance a full pot weighing at least a hundred kilos in one hand with an empty one in the other hand, without spilling a drop.

Then he put the first one down and picked up the third with that hand, holding it at arm's length while he drank the entire contents of the second pot, then switched hands and drained most of the third as well. It was one of those mornings.

He dropped the third empty pot to the ground with a resounding echo and patted his flat abdomen, making a show of turning around as he pulled off his upper garment and pulled on a fresh one. He saw the Hijras' eyes widen and noted their exchange of looks and secret gestures: touching one finger tip to another, the jerk of a chin in a certain direction, the rolling of the head at an angle. They were expressing astonishment at how any being could consume that much water without revealing any sign of it upon his body. They had no notion that Kamsa could read their secret language – it was one of the things he had picked up during his stint with Jarasandha's army, and had been shrewd enough to keep to himself. Good to be able to interpret the secret coded communications of your enemy; better yet to be able to do so without their knowing you can do so. They were surely aware of how he had despatched four of their comrades in this very chamber not many moons ago: he sensed that awareness in their eyes as well. That was why they had been relatively polite with him. Had they thought him merely human, they would have hauled him away like an errant dog. But now, word of that incident coupled with their watching him drink close to three hundred litres of water without his belly expanding by even a millimetre had earned their respect. They were impressed despite themselves: that was saying something, for Jarasandha's Hijras weren't easy to impress.

Kamsa smiled. 'I believe I shall eat before we leave,' he said aloud. 'I have a great appetite in the mornings.' He felt ravenous enough to put away at least as much food as he had drunk water and didn't wait for them to protest. He doubted they had ever seen anyone consume two or three hundred kilos of food without showing any sign of it on the body. Now he had a feeling that the Hijras would think very carefully before disrespecting or questioning his authority. To complete the victory, he said casually: 'Do join me at table.'

The journey was by boat. Jarasandha was stationed a few score yojanas upriver. By the same time the next day, Jarasandha would have moved on to another city, another battle; and it could take days to reach him. That was why Kamsa had to be brought to him on the same day. The boat was like nothing

Kamsa had seen before. The Yadavas, like most Aryas, were not seafaring or even river-faring people. They preferred travelling with solid ground underfoot. But he had heard of cultures further south in Aryavarta where entire nations used river concourses the way most others used roads. He assumed that this craft was of their design. Long, sinuous as a serpent, it stretched for at least four score yards, maybe a few more, and was about barely seven or eight yards wide. There were two rows of eunuchs with unusual, long rowing poles on each side of the boat's length, perhaps eighty on each side. The craft's sides curved upwards from the water as if seeking to complete a circle. Running the length of the centre of the craft from one end to the other was a platform elevated about a yard from the boat's inner base. Upon this were affixed seats and tables. Foremen walked the length of this platform, wielding whips. The quad that had fetched Kamsa led him aboard the snake boat without a word to anyone and indicated a seat for him to rest. He eschewed the seat and remained standing, wishing to see how such a craft was worked.

The foreman at the end of the boat called out a command and the teams of Hijras came alert at once, taking up their oars. A drummer began a martial beat, slow but precise, and the foreman gave commands to the rowers to angle their oars, then to begin rowing. Kamsa felt the surge of power as the boat leapt forward almost at once, against the current. The eunuchs' powerful muscles glistened in the morning sunlight as they worked rhythmically in perfect unison. A foreman or two cracked a whip in the air beside the ear of anyone not able to keep perfect rhythm and the marginal error was corrected instantly. Knowing how disciplined Jarasandha's Hijras were raised to be, Kamsa thought that there would be few occasions to actually punish them with those whips. Their efficiency and coordination were quite extraordinary. He had never thought it possible to move upriver at this point in the Yamuna's course at such a pace. Yet the snake boat's canny design and construction, coupled with the Hijras' excellent rowing were carrying them forward at a pace even a four-horse chariot team would be hard-pressed to match. He saw Yadava soldiers, commoners and children pointing and gesturing at the boat as it sped past them, and developed a new admiration for his father-in-law's shrewd military mind. It was the use of such ingenuity and ramrod discipline that made Jarasandha the most formidable conqueror in this part of the world.

Several hours later, the river widened briefly to one of its enormous delta-like patches. The flow was relatively slower here, but the width of the course was enormous, almost a full kilometre from bank to bank. There were small islands in the middle of the river, and he could see armed men on each of them.

As they approached their destination, Kamsa saw the results of Jarasandha's recent campaign. There were dead bodies everywhere on the eastern bank, human as well as elephant, horse and camel. Fires burned in pockets across the land, some several yojanas away, others only a few dozen yards from the bank. From what he could make out of the closest ones, they were piles of corpses being unloaded from uks wagons and heaped on pyres. The stench of burning flesh carried for yojanas around – he had smelt it an hour before they reached this part of the river. At another point, he could make out soldiers still fighting in a clump of trees. He could see the glint of the setting sun reflecting off armour and weapons. Faint sounds of men screaming and dying came and went as they sped past. At one point, a hail of arrows came out of nowhere and splashed into the water, yards behind their boat. Kamsa was unable to tell where they had come from but a moment later a javelin, beautifully thrown, came swishing through the air and landed close to the main foreman at the front of the boat. The eunuch saw the javelin but ignored it and it missed him by perhaps an inch. No more missiles were aimed at them after this.

When their boat began to slow, Kamsa understood that they were about to disembark. He could see the unmistakable signs of a large army presence – krta-dhvaja flags flapping in the strong evening river breeze, lances reflecting sunlight as riders rode by on a nearby road, the stench of dead flesh from somewhere close, suggesting a battlefield. Most peculiar was a place they passed, a large makeshift construction from which great roars could be heard. It sounded like a stadium of some kind, with some sport in progress, and a great audience watching. He wondered what sport they might be playing, and his aching muscles began to hurt again as he remembered the old syce and the activities of the night before.

They disembarked on the eastern bank where a surprisingly large jetty served several dozen such snake boats. The constant coming and going of these vessels suggested major troop movement. Kamsa understood at least one reason why Jarasandha's enemies feared him so much: even when not engaged in conquering some new territory, his forces were never too far away from previously held kingdoms.

He was taken by chariot to a staging area a mile or two eastwards. Here, a great encampment stretched out for as far as his eye could discern. Though he had fought in Jarasandha's army years ago, Kamsa was impressed by the new scale and precision of that army's development. Then it had been an alliance of diverse kings with a common vested interest banding together in an attempt to create a unified empire. Now, it was a consolidated entity under a single emperor with his imperial host, building a world with his personal brand on it. Wherever Kamsa turned he saw only a single krta-dhvaja, and that was Jarasandha's banner. Apparently, the alliance had been reduced to a single sigil. Had the reduction been accomplished by attrition or infighting? Probably a combination of both. Jarasandha no longer needed anyone else's help or support to continue his campaign.

Guarded densely by the largest eunuchs Kamsa had ever seen, the emperor's pavilion was an impressive sight from the outside. The Hijras reminded him of those who had surrounded Jarasandha when Kamsa first went to meet him, back in Magadha. That was a long time ago and he had fought and bested a few of them through sheer arrogant luck and youthful zest. Now, he knew he could crush any of them and a part of him hoped he would have a chance to do so.

Jarasandha was seated with dignity upon a throne dais in the centre of an enormous tent whose interior rivalled the throne chamber in Mathura. He was surrounded by eunuchs as usual, Kamsa noted, many in various states of casual relaxation. These were part of Jarasandha's inner circle – the giant cross-breeds who were the best fighters of all and whom he kept close by him at all times. But that was not the only reason he kept them close. They were also his companions in other pursuits. Jarasandha's proclivities were wide and diverse and he made no secret of them.

'Son-in-law,' said the Magadhan, greeting Kamsa with his usual show of formality. 'Welcome. It is good to see you once

again. My daughters will be even more pleased. It has been a
while since they had the pleasure of your company. They are
in separate quarters quite near mine. Would you like to see
them first?'

Kamsa had expected his wives to be present. It was vital to
Jarasandha's plans of firmly entwining Mathura's destiny with
Magadha's future that Kamsa continue his bloodline by giving
him heirs. 'Perhaps later. You wished to see me urgently?'

Jarasandha gestured. Several of the eunuchs catering to the
more menial duties such as fetching food and drink or swishing
fans departed the chamber at once. The few who remained
lounged languorously on velveteen cushions, scantily clad in
garments that Kamsa would have preferred seeing on women.
Noticing Kamsa's grimace, one fellow with an egg-shaped
head and kohl-ringed eyes raised his eyebrow and smiled
provocatively. Kamsa smiled and shook his head, knowing
better than to rise to the provocation.

They were served food and drink as Jarasandha talked. The
god emperor spoke of the political situation, various factions
and links and alliances, all of which Kamsa knew of already.

'I am well aware of the politics of Bharat-varsha,' Kamsa said
at last. 'I hardly think I needed a refresher lesson, sire.'

Jarasandha's tongue flickered between his parted lips as he
tasted a particularly tasty delicacy, some variety of blackish red
crustacean that he said was a favourite savoury of the people of
that particular region. Jarasandha was known for sampling the
cuisine of every region he conquered and choosing which tribal
chieftain to permit to rule as satrap on his behalf based on his
liking the food prepared by his cooks. Kamsa noticed that the
delicacy had claws and a hard shell, and as Jarasandha popped

it into his mouth whole, the loud crunching sound left no doubt that it was some variety of riverbed crawler. He thought of advising Jarasandha that the item in question was supposed to be eaten after one cracked open the shell, then realized the point was moot. He picked out one for himself and popped it in. The crunchy sensation was actually quite pleasurable. It occurred to him that his newfound ability enabled him to eat things he might otherwise have found indigestible. He wondered if his new digestion could process anything his mouth could break down. It might be interesting to try.

'I heard of Putana's death,' Jarasandha said, sending his forked tongue flickering out to clean the whole of his upper lip and then his chin. 'And that you did not take it too well.'

Kamsa shrugged. 'I was upset but not any more.' He looked Jarasandha directly in the eyes, knowing that as father of his wives, the god emperor might forgive infidelity on Kamsa's part, but not emotional attachment. 'The woman herself meant nothing to me. It was her failure that upset me.'

Jarasandha held his gaze a moment longer. If eyes could seek as widely as the Magadhan's tongue could reach, Jarasandha would have looked inside Kamsa's belly and sought the truth within his bowels. As it was, his response seemed to satisfy Jarasandha, who nodded, suddenly seeming relieved. 'Of course. Failure in one's soldiers is unacceptable. But you have other assassins out seeking the Slayer.'

Of course Jarasandha knew he had other assassins at work: each one of them was given to him by Jarasandha himself. Kamsa nodded. 'Each of them is capable of storming a citadel, let alone killing an infant.'

Jarasandha picked out another delicacy from a different platter, no doubt the preparation of another tribe's best cook.

'Yet this is no mere infant. To slay the Slayer is no simple mission.'

He popped in the item and took two bites before making a face and using a silk napkin to spit out the uneaten morsel. Clearly, that tribe was not going to be holding much sway over political matters in the region.

Kamsa sipped his wine, forcing himself not to gulp it down. It had already been several hours since he had eaten and he was ravenous. At least the aches and pains from the night before had reduced somewhat. That old fellow! 'Yet Putana assured me that even this Slayer can be defeated.'

Jarasandha nodded. 'It may well be so. But we shall know soon enough, shall we not? I am sure the other assassins are making their move against him even as we speak.' He gestured dismissively. 'The reason I called you here is because I wish that you leave off this campaign against the Slayer.'

Kamsa stopped with his goblet in hand, mid-sip. He looked at Jarasandha and put down the goblet. 'Leave off? What do you mean, sire?'

'Leave it to the assassins. In any case, they will probably succeed in ridding you of the problem. But—'

'But what?'

'But in the event they fail as well, it might be best if you do not pursue this course further for the time being.'

Kamsa leaned forward. 'Are you telling me that I should let the child prophesied to grow up to become my murderer live free? That I should sit here and do nothing about it?'

'Not here, exactly. I would have you sit upon the throne of Mathura,' Jarasandha said. 'After all, I helped put you on that throne, did I not?'

'Yes, and I am grateful for that, Father-in-law,' Kamsa said.

'But this is a personal matter. I cannot simply let it go, as you suggest.'

'It is personal, that is why I am asking this of you. You are a king now and a king must look beyond his immediate personal interests to the larger issues.'

'Such as …?'

'Such as the rising unrest in your kingdom. The increasing emigration of the Yadavas to other nations such as Bhoja. The discomfort of your neighbours and other powerful states about your inability to govern without civil disobedience.'

'Ah!' Kamsa understood at last. 'You are concerned that I may harry the Vrishnis and provoke a civil war. If that happens, you're worried about Bhoja supporting the rebels … and other states joining in the melee as well. That's what you're really worried about, isn't it?'

Jarasandha stopped eating, leaned back in his throne and looked at Kamsa speculatively. He was as lean and ramrod thin as ever, his slender appearance belying his physical strength and fighting skills. 'I see you have improved your knowledge of political science.'

Kamsa smiled. 'I had an excellent guru.'

Jarasandha burst into laughter. The eunuchs turned their heads in surprise: clearly, they weren't accustomed to their god emperor being amused by his visitors. 'And diplomacy too! Well, well. Who would have thought it? Kamsa the boy wonder suddenly growing hair on his brain!'

Kamsa took up his goblet of wine again and drank deeply. 'You have nothing to worry about. I will not make any rash moves against the Vrishnis. There will be no retaliation for the killing of Putana. Even if the other assassins fail,' he paused, forcing himself not to admit how much that prospect angered him, 'I will not pursue any direct course of action for the time being. I know how delicate the political situation is right now. A single misstep could set the rebellion ablaze. Once the Yadavas go to civil war, it can only end with my death. Better to let the Slayer go for now and deal with him later than risk my own countrymen rising against me and destroying me.'

Jarasandha nodded approvingly. 'You see it clearly then. You might well rid yourself of one future Slayer only to create a whole nation of slayers who want you dead. Better to bide your time. Your day against the Slayer will come, I am sure of it. And when it does, I have no doubt that you will be ready to face him, whoever he might be.'

There was an instant when Kamsa saw something flicker in Jarasandha's eyes as his nictitating eyelids panned shut sideways, then opened again. Could it possibly be? Could Jarasandha know the identity of the Slayer? If so, why would he not tell Kamsa? Surely it was in Jarasandha's own interest to keep Kamsa alive and powerful?

Then he remembered what the old man had told him the night before – that morning, actually. And he thought to himself, yes, it was possible, even likely, that Jarasandha knew the identity of the Slayer but chose to keep it to himself. After all, the three surviving assassins were all Jarasandha's men, hand-picked by him for that very mission. They must surely be sending word back to him somehow.

It did not matter. In any case, Jarasandha and Kamsa needed one another, not merely to join their bloodlines and give Jarasandha's grandchildren the legitimacy he lacked, but as political allies too. If Jarasandha knew who the Slayer was, he would do everything in his power to destroy the child before he grew stronger. About that, even the syce had no two opinions.

Jarasandha rose from his seat. 'Enough talk,' he said imperiously. 'Come now. Let us try some sport.'

'Sport?' Kamsa asked, frowning as he rose. He set the goblet down. 'What sport do you have in mind?'

Jarasandha smiled, his snake eyes flickering mischievously. 'Something that will require all your newfound ability to survive. Come, let me show you.'

eleven

Yashoda cried out as the thicket erupted in an explosion of leaves, dust and wind. There was no warning or indication of anything untoward even a moment earlier. It was as if a whirlwind suddenly descended out of the clear sky and struck the very spot where she stood. The air churned at a great speed, lifting up countless particles of dust and tiny debris. She was forced to cover her eyes with the back of her hand. The wind whipped around her, tugging her this way then that, threatening to topple her over. Trees roared above, the wind shirring their leaves like a storm. Monkeys and birds went berserk and screamed and cried out in terror. The whole world turned brownish grey, the colour of fading autumn leaves. She struggled to stay on her feet even as she tried to find her way back to the sala tree.

Krishna! I must get to Krishna!

But the instant she moved a step downhill, the wind increased in intensity, whipping her face with greater savagery. She stepped back, moving away from the direction of the tree and her son, and instantly felt the difference. The tree was the centre of the unnatural storm. Her heart flooded with terror. She turned and stared uphill. She could still see Nanda silhouetted against the clear blue sky. He was staring down in disbelief. As she watched, he roused himself and started sprinting down towards her.

The storm is only here, in this spot, nowhere else.

She knew what that meant – this was another attempt on her son's life.

Krishna!

She took another step downhill and was buffeted back so hard, it felt like a mule had kicked her in the midriff. She fell back, staggering, and uncovered her eyes for a second as she flailed out to try and keep her balance. The dust blinded her. She cried out in pain and terror and grasped hold of something that felt like the trunk of a neem tree. She held on to it for safety as the roaring of the wind increased and it roared and howled like a thousand savage beasts out for blood. She made another attempt to move towards the spot where she knew Krishna was but it was quite impossible. She would either be blinded or worse: there were branches and small stones being flung about by the whirlwind. One thumped her in the back, knocking the breath out of her. She knew that if she tried to go closer again, she would be killed.

Even that was not enough to stop her. The real problem was that she knew she couldn't pick up Krishna and run away with him. That was the reason why she had been separated for him for those few moments. The reason why she had been about to ask Nanda to come to her and try to figure out a solution. Somehow, Krishna had increased his weight to the point where he weighed too much for her to carry.

The whirlwind grew more intense, the dust and debris striking her all over now, hurting terribly. She kept her eyes shut and hugged the neem tree, using it to shield herself as best as she could. Stones and branches struck her incessantly from behind and one blow from a sharp rock on the back of her head made her vision turn black for a moment, but she clung on fiercely. Though she could see or hear nothing, she knew that this was no mere natural phenomenon. This was some kind of asura taking the form of the wind. A demon whirlwind. She knew it as surely as she knew the reason why Krishna had increased his weight. Not to trouble her and make it impossible for her to carry him – or perhaps just enough to force her to put him down, so that she would not be with him when the wind demon struck – but in order to make it harder for the demon to pick him up and spirit him away.

Harder.

But not impossible.

As she clung to the tree trunk for dear life, Yashoda felt the whirlwind ratchet up to a new level of intensity, turning the world around her blackish grey, and felt even the tree she was holding on to begin to uproot. It shuddered violently, and in that instant, she thought that it was the end, she was about to die and there was nothing she could do to save herself or her little baby.

Although, perhaps, he might be able to save her.

'Krishna!' she cried out, just as the neem tree tore free of its roots in a terrible rending agony, and she felt herself lifted off the ground and flung up into the air.

twelve

The roar of thousands filled the air and though the place was open to the night air, the stench of sweat was overwhelming. Torches burned at regular intervals and Kamsa could see their flames flicker as the crowd stomped its feet and rose and sat in enthusiasm as it cheered on the fighters. The stadium was a quadrangle and in the centre was a grassy ground cleared of all stones, rocks and impediments. This rectangular field was divided into two halves and clearly marked with chalk dust lines. Within the two halves of this rectangle stood perhaps forty men. Kamsa squinted. Yes, exactly forty men, twenty on each side of the middle line. The two teams faced each other, spread out across their respective halves in defensive formations. All the men were stripped bare, wearing only a dusty langot – the little strip of cloth used to cover one's privates – tied around the waist by a string. Their bodies were well oiled. Kamsa noted boys standing on the sidelines, ready to rush in and apply more oil to the players' bodies as needed, others redrawing the chalk lines where they had been rubbed out during play.

'The goal is simple: to get to the enemy's innermost line – its home line.' Jarasandha pointed to the two lines behind the teams, the short sides of the rectangle. 'The enemy team's players can stop you using any means, but if any of them are touching you when you touch their home line, they are eliminated from the game. For every enemy player you eliminate from the game, you are entitled to bring back one of your own players who was eliminated earlier – or, if he is too badly hurt to continue, you can bring a replacement. Players attempt to cross to enemy lines one at a time at first, but each successful contact with the home line entitles a player to return with a comrade to try his luck again, and so on.'

Kamsa nodded. 'And the game ends when all the enemy players are eliminated or all your players have touched the enemy's home line.'

Jarasandha's thin lips curled in a half-smile. 'I see you're familiar with the game.'

'It's a variation on an old war game that has been played for millennia. It's based on the ancient game of chaupat. The war game of strategy.'

Jarasandha's smile widened. 'So it is. How interesting. I'm delighted to see that your education has expanded since we last met. Very pleased indeed. Of course, there's one essential difference between this version of the game and chaupat.'

Kamsa waited for Jarasandha to deliver the punch line he knew was coming.

'Chaupat is played with bone dice and pieces on a board of squares. It's a game for idle kings and merchants who have money to wager and time to spare but don't wish to exert themselves. Kho kabaddi is played with real opponents and involves real bodily harm.'

Jarasandha directed Kamsa towards a section of the stadium not immediately visible. Kamsa looked over a railing that enclosed a small area just outside the playing quadrant, beneath the rows of wooden seats on which the crowd sat. Several dozen bodies were piled there, limbs and heads and torsos grotesquely twisted and bent at impossible angles. Many of them still had their eyes open, faces twisted in a rictus of agony, and Kamsa saw one particularly large and well-built specimen staring up at him blankly, his eyes reflecting the flickering light of the torch near Kamsa's head.

Jarasandha patted Kamsa's shoulder patronizingly. 'I encourage bouts between my soldiers and men from the opposing army every night. It helps build morale. How would you like to try your luck?'

Kamsa heard himself say, 'I wouldn't mind having a go.'

He turned back to Jarasandha and smiled. Jarasandha chuckled and patted him on his back again. 'That's the spirit, my boy!'

Kamsa knew that Jarasandha thought he knew what was about to happen – but he also knew that Jarasandha was unaware that Kamsa knew what Jarasandha had planned, or the fact that Kamsa had come prepared for this very event. Thanks to the old syce in Mathura.

thirteen

Krishna was asleep. Ever since the attack by Matrika Putana, he had been sleeping more than usual. The reason was the milk he had consumed. As Putana had grown larger in size, enlarging herself to gargantuan proportions, so also had the milk flowing from her glands increased in quantum. Krishna had consumed a great quantity of that poisonous substance. Several times his body weight, in fact. Powerful as he was, he was subject to certain basic limitations of the form he used in this world. The form of a mortal human infant did not allow for much leeway: the poison was far, far more than he could absorb or digest in this body. His only recourse was to call upon his cosmic powers and divert the poison to the ethereal sphere. To the infinite form of Vishnu himself, seated on the great serpent Ananta, floating on the ocean of milk. In that timeless state of nidra super-consciousness, the matrika's poison milk was nothing to him. He could turn it into anything he desired. But Vishnu was preoccupied with a great many matters and although Krishna was his own amsa, literally a part of himself in human form, not merely an avatar, he could allot only so much of his attention and energy to this task. It also transpired that Vishnu was currently engaged in a great conflict between the devas and asuras, a new skirmish in the infinite war between the two celestial factions. Therefore, he was able to give his Krishna self only a portion of his energy and time. Krishna was forced to do all the work himself, pushing the poison to his original father-self, and was limited by the weakness of his human infant form in this work. Vishnu could have sucked the poison up to the ocean of milk in an instant, cleansing Krishna in the wink of an eye, and he would do so the instant he was free, but days and now weeks had passed on earth and Vishnu's involvement in the asura–deva struggle and other matters had only increased since then. So Krishna the infant concentrated all his energies towards pushing the poison up to vaikunthaloka. This drained him considerably. That was the reason why he had not been able to speak mentally to Maatr Yashoda and reassure her since the incident. Most perplexing of all was the inexplicable urge he had developed to consume dahi, a substance he knew of but which was hardly appropriate for an infant of his tender age. He could hardly wait until he was old enough to ask Yashoda to feed him dahi in all possible forms: lassi, most of all! Even freshly churned butter would do, as would whipped curd. Yum! Even the thought made him open his mouth and long for it.

But now there was something else amiss. He was still asleep, exhausted from a long session of pushing the poison heavenwards, but he had sensed something ominous unfolding around him, which is why he had allowed his weight to increase, in order to compel Yashoda-maiya to put him down. He knew that the demon was coming: he could smell him approaching long before he reached. The demon had been watching and biding his time for weeks now, ever since Putana's death, and had seen his opportunity at last. Yashoda was relatively unescorted, with only the bodyguards several yards away, and there was an open field of attack.

Even when Yashoda had put Krishna down, and his head had lolled back against the tree trunk and the trunk had cracked, Krishna had been aware of what was going on. While the human part of him was fast asleep, the divine part still knew that Yashoda was in grave danger. So he sent an impulse into Nanda-baba's mind, causing him to come to the top of the hill and call out to Yashoda. This in turn made Yashoda leave Krishna alone for a moment, long enough for the demon to see his opportunity and make his move. Krishna was concerned that the demon would attack while Yashoda was still with him, in which case, she might be harmed. This way, she was several yards away at least. He would have preferred that she be miles away but this was the next best thing. As the whirlwind exploded around him and the dust and debris enveloped him in a blinding miasma of madness, he sensed Yashoda clinging to the neem tree nearby. She was being buffeted and battered but she would survive unharmed. Now he could focus on managing the demon.

The creature in question was a being named Trnavarta. Krishna was not familiar with him personally but he had sensed this particular being's presence – his supernatural stench, actually – for some time now. He had been part of the group that had arrived in Vraj with Putana, one of the team of assassins sent by his uncle. But, in fact, Trnavarta was not Kamsa's man at all. His loyalty was pledged to Jarasandha, who was a demon himself, and a very powerful one at that. Krishna knew Jarasandha well – or rather, Vishnu knew him, which was the same thing.

Jarasandha was a bad man. A bad, bad man.

Some day, Krishna would have to confront him too. He knew this for certain just as he knew that Jarasandha was using and manipulating Kamsa to further his own ends. But right now, Krishna was facing Trnavarta and had to deal with him.

He opened his inner eye and looked at Trnavarta.

Not his human infant eyes – they would be blinded by the dust and grit, perhaps injured severely – he opened his celestial eye, which enabled him to view things as they truly were, looking beyond the obvious superficial appearance and physicality.

He saw himself at the apex of a vortex. Dust, debris, grit, even little stones and twigs and branches, all swirling round in a frenzy. The sala tree was being systematically stripped of its leaves and branches, and even its bark was peeling off and being swallowed by the vortex. The funnel of the whirlwind was focussed upon his little human form at the base of the tree, as Trnavarta tried to lift him up in the air. Thus far, he was not having much luck and this was frustrating him. He whipped himself faster, churning the air in a circular motion, reducing the radius of his vortex to increase the intensity. This made the funnel narrower, which was good for Krishna because the intensity of the churning air was reduced even further outside of the centre.

Krishna sensed Yashoda-maiya stumbling and breaking away from the neem tree instinctively, her eyes still shut. Nanda came running downhill just then, took hold of Yashoda and led her a few yards farther away from the centre of the chaos. The bodyguards were nearby too, one holding his head where something had slashed it open, blood pouring down his face and eyes, but there was nothing he could do. This was not some woman they could pull away from Krishna or even an assassin with a knife or a sword. Krishna observed Yashoda and Nanda speaking agitatedly to one another, trying to peer through the murky storm by the sala tree, then debating with the bodyguards. Other people had come to the top of the hill, alerted by Nanda's shouts, and word began to spread as people realized what was going on. The music over the hill ceased and people stopped their ras-lila dancing to deal with the new crisis. Krishna hoped they would keep their distance. In his present weakened state, he was not sure how much he could do to protect them.

Now that he had checked on Yashoda and Nanda and knew that they were safe, he turned his attention to Trnavarta. Where was the asura? With all the dust and debris flying about, it was difficult to make out the demon himself. At first, all Krishna could see was a funnel of grit spinning to a height of twenty or thirty yards above the ground. It enveloped the entire sala tree, making it seem as if the tree itself were spinning around. Krishna sent his consciousness up the length of the tree to the top.

There.

At the very top was the demon, a distinctly masculine figure standing upright. Though he took the form of human flesh on earth, his body was made of molecules of pure asura maya, and he possessed the power to spin these molecules around the way a dancer in swirling robes could spin until the robes swirled around as well, rising in the air. Right now, he was almost entirely in his demon form, his upper body only barely discernible, his face contorted with murderous rage and effort. His mouth was open and a howling sound exuded from it, a keening sound like the wind. His torso looked like a great wad of cloth tightly wound into a knot, the bottom of the knot splaying out into myriad threads that merged with the grey funnel of the vortex. At a glance, it looked a little like a man in a grey frock suit twirling while playing ras-lila. The thought made Krishna giggle a little.

Trnavarta heard or sensed the laughter and his eyes widened. Motes of matter broke free from his eyes and face and went spinning down to join the vortex. His face lost its integrity as his anger rose. He opened his mouth and howled in response.

Foolish child! You dare titter at me?

Sorry, mister asura. I can't help it if you look so funny! You look like a ras-garbha dancer in a flowing skirt, turning round and round. Don't you feel dizzy, spinning so fast?

Trnavarta roared and lashed out with one arm. A branch of his spinning vortex reached out and swiped at the place where Krishna's inner eye hung suspended in mid-air above the tree, looking down. Krishna felt a sensation like a blast of wind and grit coming at him but, of course, his inner eye was insubstantial and could not be touched or harmed. Trnavarta realized this at once and roared again, in frustration this time. His upper body shook in anger, making him look like a dancer who had suddenly missed a step and was angry with himself for his own clumsiness.

This made Krishna laugh even more, because it did look quite funny.

Silence, you brat! I will silence you forever for your impudence.

Krishna stopped laughing and smiled. *You may certainly try. But before you do, why not go someplace where we have more space to settle this? Some place higher, perhaps? The whole sky is empty and available for us.*

Krishna saw Trnavarta look down at the base of the tree below him and at the physical body of little Krishna seated there, still apparently asleep. Then he looked up at the sky. He nodded slowly, a wily look coming over his wind-ravaged face.

Perhaps we shall. I know you have deliberately made your body heavier in the hope that I wouldn't be able to lift you high and drop you down from a height. Until now, I have been unable to lift your body itself, no doubt due to your unique nature. But if I cannot touch your body and lift it up, I can raise up the ground on which it rests. The ground is not possessed of any divine power and so cannot resist me!

And with a great burst of laughter, Trnavarta reached down with his insubstantial grey body and began to rip up a section of the ground around the sala tree. Within moments, he had torn free a roughly circular patch several dozen yards around, with the sala tree in the centre. He exerted a visible effort, a little strain showing on his face, then yanked hard, ripping the little island free of its earthly tethering. Roots and rocks fell free as the patch of ground rose up into the air.

Krishna felt his body jerk as it was lifted up in the air. With astonishing speed, Trnavarta carried him up in the air, up to the sky as he himself had suggested. He was surprised. He had only suggested the idea because he had been certain Trnavarta could not lift him. The asura's demoniac nature made it impossible for him to manhandle Krishna's divinely infused human form. But by uprooting the whole patch of earth, Trnavarta had outwitted him.

fourteen

Kamsa finished oiling his body and dismissed the helper. The boy ran back to the sidelines to join his companions who were whispering amongst themselves as they pointed out the players on the field. Kamsa saw some coins exchanging hands and grinned to himself. He wondered whom they were betting on. He felt certain that it would be Jarasandha's team of champions. Kamsa had been given the choice of playing with Jarasandha's or the opposing army's team, and knowing it would irk his father-in-law and provoke him into trying harder, he had chosen to play with the opposing team. Jarasandha still believed he was surprising his son-in-law into mistakenly thinking he would be able to use his powers to easily demolish his opponents on this field, not knowing that each of the players was possessed of his own powers as well. But Kamsa knew this already. He knew because the old stable syce had told him so the night before – not merely told him to warn him, but had prepared him for it as well.

Yadu, that is his name. I should think of him by that name.

After all, Kamsa mused, the man was no mere stablehand. He was none other than Yadu himself. The founding father of the Yadava nation and forebear of Kamsa's entire line.

'Do you know who I am?' the old man had demanded when he moved against Kamsa the night before, his fingers grasping Kamsa's throat in a grip so tight, Kamsa could feel his breath choked off. This was impossible because once he increased his body's density, it was no less than a thing made of solid iron or lead. Yet the old man was strong enough to crush even a throat made of iron. Kamsa was incredulous.

'I am Yadu,' said the old syce, his breath wafting hot against Kamsa's face, redolent of the last meal he had eaten. 'I am the forebear of your race, boy. I have lived long enough to see this nation grow from a single family of exiles into the proud Yadava nation it is today. And yes, as you are probably wondering, I am stronger than you. For the ability you have developed, though it was unwittingly awakened by Jarasandha's potions, its essence is in your very blood itself. *My* blood!'

Then the old man had released Kamsa with a shove and he had stumbled back against the stable wall, striking it with force enough to make the entire structure shudder and groan. The horses whinnied in alarm, smelling the aggression in the air, reacting to it. The more aggressive ones stamped their feet and kicked the rear of their stalls impatiently. Yadu turned his back on Kamsa, walking a few steps away.

'I have watched from the sidelines these past centuries as your ancestors, my descendants, built a kingdom and a nation that I was very proud of. Even Ugrasena, your father, was a good king. Though in his youth he did tend to warmonger more than he needed to, he more than made up for it by realizing the futility of violence and addressing his past excesses by seeking peace with his allies, our fellow Suras. After all, whether you live on this bank of the Yamuna or the other side, you are all Yadavas, children of Yadu. And I was glad to see peace finally settle across this war-harried land. But then you came along and revealed your inner demon. And everything fell apart!'

Kamsa regained his voice and glared at the old syce. 'You mean to tell me that you have lived here as a stablehand for these hundreds of years and nobody knew it? You, the forebear of the Yadava race himself?'

Yadu shrugged. 'They thought me dead a long time ago. They even mistook a body for mine on the battlefield and assumed it was too mutilated to recognize. It happens. Sons are impatient to inherit, people are always happy to have change ...' He shook his head, sighing. 'The very origin of our line began that way, with my father disowning me.' He looked up and saw Kamsa staring up at him blankly. 'It is not an incident much written about in Yadava histories because it was not our proudest moment, to know that our line began because I was exiled from my father's house for my inability to do as he asked.'

Kamsa came forward warily, rubbing his throat. 'What did he ask? Who was your father?'

Yadu shrugged. 'His name was Yayati and he wanted to exchange his old age for my youth ...'

'Exchange ...?' Kamsa couldn't understand what the man meant. He was still having a hard time processing the idea that this old stable sweeper was his ancestor, the progenitor of his entire lineage.

Yadu made a dismissive gesture. 'It's a long story which I shall tell you some other time. Right now, there is a reason why I am revealing my true identity to you.'

Kamsa waited to hear it.

Yadu told him. It was a very good reason. Listening to it made Kamsa forget all about the pain in his throat. It almost made him stop wanting to lunge at Yadu and tear the old man apart limb from limb for having done what he had to him.

Now, Kamsa stepped out on the field and began slapping his muscles to warm them up. He slapped his chest hard several times, then massaged his shoulders, swung his torso around to loosen the back muscles, bent and slapped his inner thighs, outer thighs … He felt a shadow approach, looming over him. In the background, the sound of the crowd was a tangible thing, all pervasive, filling the air like rain on water.

'Yadava!' said a great booming voice. For a moment Kamsa thought he must be hearing an echo caused by the enclosed stadium. Then he looked up into a jaw the size of his own thigh and realized that it was not an echo, merely the natural sound produced by a person of that size. The man's chest was probably twice as wide as Kamsa's, and Kamsa was not a small man by any standards. He was also a good two heads taller and his arms hung by his sides like entire hams of meat. His jaw was square and jutted out at an angle, forcing his lower teeth up over the upper ones. When he spoke, the sound was like someone speaking inside a wooden barrel filled with metal ingots.

'Our master tells me you consider yourself invulnerable,' said the grating barrel voice.

Kamsa did not answer. The man's tone made it clear he was more interested in issuing insults than actually conversing. This was a common precursor to games as each team boosted its own spirit by insulting the other team and calling it names. He had expected no less.

The man seemed to realize that an answer was not forthcoming from Kamsa.

'Well, since you consider yourself invulnerable,' he said, 'I wanted to show you this.'

The man drew a sword. It was a fine broadsword, fit for any high lord or even a king in battle, the metal beautifully worked and beaten to a fine perfection. Judging by the size and length and the make, it could probably hack through armour if wielded hard enough; it might take a swing or three but no armour could withstand more than a few direct hits with that weapon. It was what the Yadava marauders called a Godslayer.

The man with the crooked jaw raised the sword in his hand, then hacked down at his own forearm, the inner softer side. The Godslayer struck his forearm with force enough to part metal armour.

The sword simply struck the forearm with a dull thunk.

The man raised his eyes to see if Kamsa had noted this result. Then he raised the sword again and hacked at his own foot, aiming directly at the knee, the weakest part of any man's leg. The sword struck with a dull thumping impact again. There was no effect on the man's knee. Even the skin wasn't broken.

The demonstration went on a few moments longer. By the time Crooked Jaw was done, the sword was chipped and cracked in a dozen places, but there was not so much as a blemish upon his person.

Finally, he handed the sword to another of his companions, a broad shorter man with enormous bulging shoulders who grinned to display missing teeth. 'That is Maitrey,' said Crooked Jaw in his booming nasal voice. 'He eats only nails and glass. I am Mustika.'

Kamsa did not say a word.

Crooked Jaw looked down at him and smiled grimly. 'You thought you were the only one, did you not? Well, you were wrong. We are all the same, and we have far more experience and knowledge of our abilities than you, sweet-faced prince. You should go back to your sweet-smelling kingdom and resume prancing with your ponies and princesses. This is no place for you.'

Kamsa cleared his throat. 'King.'

Crooked Jaw frowned.

'I am king of Mathura, lord of the Yadavas.'

Crooked Jaw grinned. 'I hear your Yadavas have fled to other kingdoms rather than be ruled by you. Is that why you come here? To grovel at our master's feet in the hope that he will aid you again and give you more of his potions to drink so that you may gain more abilities?' He leaned closer and chuckled. 'Or perhaps you needed something to aid you in bed with his daughters? Word is that you have not been able to seed either of them with child for years. Perhaps you require some help? I would be happy to help any time. As would all my teammates. Just say the word.'

Kamsa reached out a hand, indicating the sword.

Crooked Jaw raised an eyebrow but handed the sword over without comment.

Kamsa took the sword, turned it inwards, the point of the blade aimed at his own lower abdomen and, gripping the hilt in both hands, said, 'When I am done here on this field today, you and all your teammates will wish you were my wives and could feel the pleasure of mating with me.'

Crooked Jaw's eyes narrowed and his fists clenched.

Kamsa went on. 'And if you survive, I would be happy to seed you with child if you wish as well. I have more than enough to seed all your nation's women as well as men.'

And he plunged the sword's point into the weakest point of any man's abdomen, hard enough to pierce wood.

The sword cracked and broke into three separate pieces.

Kamsa handed the hilt back to Crooked Jaw who stared at the broken blade. 'You can keep this one. I prefer my own.'

He smiled to himself as Crooked Jaw, striding back to his side, flung the pieces of the broken sword across the field, yelling at his startled teammates. He knew his own words had been somewhat bombastic to say the least, but it was the only way to get the point across.

fifteen

Krishna looked down with his inner eye and saw the ground receding far below. He could make out the hill and all the revellers in their gaily coloured ras-lila outfits staring up and pointing as they saw what was happening. He could see Yashoda-maiya and Nanda-baba run forward, arms outstretched, crying out, agitated, and could feel their anguish and pain as they saw their child being spirited away by the wind demon. He saw the bodyguards roaring with ineffectual anger and waving their muscular arms and lathis about impotently. He felt sorry for them all, for such events were so far beyond their power to control, they might as well be ants trampled underfoot by an elephant.

He looked down at the sala tree, still embedded in the island of earth that Trnavarta had uprooted from the hillside. His physical self still sat at the foot of the tree, soundly asleep. The little babe's mouth was puckered, his curls falling across his forehead, his chubby limbs sprawled, head tilted, as he slept on, blissfully unaware of the goings-on around him. Krishna had chosen to let his physical self sleep through the crisis. The human part of him needed the rest and in any case, there was nothing he could do. He was too young to run or jump or fight or wield a weapon. Whatever course of action he chose, it would have to use the power of the mind far more than the power of the body. Some day, his human form would be strong and powerful enough, and then he could meld more of his divinity with it to use in such circumstances. But right now, he was a babe in arms. And even a feisty babe in arms is still a babe.

Trnavarta was gloating at his triumph.

How do you fancy this, god-child? Do you like the view from here? Would you like to return to earth? To your maatr and pitr?

The asura tilted the patch of ground, and even though his cosmic form was unaffected by the action, Krishna felt his human form shift with the tilt. The very weight he had added to his body to anchor it to the ground would cause it to topple over and roll off the island in a trice now. He saw his head roll from one side to the other, striking the trunk as it moved and cracking the sala tree again.

A sharper tilt and I wager your little infant self will roll right off this flying clod! Trnavarta laughed, grey grit particles exploding from his mouth and swirling around him like a swarm of flies. Perhaps now you realize that increasing your weight thousand fold was not enough to stop me from ending your short existence on this plane!

The demon was right. Whether Krishna increased or decreased his weight now would make no difference. All the asura had to do was tilt the flying island, or turn it over, and the babe lying beneath the sala tree would plummet to the ground. He glanced down: the ground in question was already several hundred yards distant and moving farther away. A fall from that height would certainly kill his physical form. And while a man might have been able to hold on to something to keep from falling off, a babe could not do so for long. Even if he could, it was not a real solution. Trnavarta had him at a disadvantage and he knew it. As before, the only way out of this was through the use of mental muscle.

Have you ever looked into a god's mind, Demon?

Trnavarta turned his inchoate head to stare at him. His face was still made up of countless particles, unable to reform itself into a cohesive whole so long as he exerted his wind powers, but there was enough face still left to form and exhibit expressions. He looked suspicious.

Do not try to trick me, Haridev. I know you devas. When you cannot win a battle by fair means, you do whatever it takes to achieve your end.

You cannot kill me.

Trnavarta shook his head, grinning.

See for yourself, Slayer of Kamsa. One sudden tilt and you will be dead ten times over! Not even the Sanjivani mantra will be able to revive you because your limbs and parts will be flung so far apart, nobody will be able to find all the pieces.

If you do not believe me, look inside my mouth.

Trnavarta spread his hands. The tips of his fingers were flowing molecules of grit streaming downwards in an endless cascade. Krishna wondered how the wind demon's disintegrating body kept scattering but never depleted fully: then he glanced up and understood. The wind brought back each molecule to its proper place. Hence the cyclical form of the attack: a whirlwind or tornado spun around, which meant that each mote or particle eventually returned to its original place. Trnavarta was constantly unmaking and remaking himself, particle by particle. Like one hand pouring a fistful of sand into the other hand's palm, then back to the first hand again, and so on, endlessly, but without spilling a grain.

Why should I bother? I have you now. You cannot escape me. You know this. I know this. Why should I listen to your godly blather? My mission is to kill you and I am about to succeed.

You are not. You will fail. That is the reason why I ask you to do this. Your arrogance is your undoing. You are making an assumption founded on a lie. You believe that if you destroy my physical body, you will kill me.

Trnavarta nodded. Yes, because it is in that physical form that you have taken birth as the Slayer.

But you are wrong. Do you think I would entrust such a great mission to a mere infant? That I would pour all my infinite power into the body of a babe? What would the point be? He cannot wield a sword, let fly an arrow, fling a spear … What kind of Slayer is he?

Trnavarta frowned. Yet you killed Putana.

That was different. She came to me as a wet nurse and tried to use that to kill me. But the poison only made me stronger.

Trnavarta's eyes widened to twice their size, particles filling in that portion of his wind-swept face to make them look almost like human eyes staring out from the whirlwind. Is that true? I have heard rumours about Putana's poison. Bahuka says that Kamsa's strength was derived from it.

Bahuka is right. I cannot be destroyed. I killed Putana and I will kill you as well, unless you release me soon and go your way and promise never to make an attempt on my life again.

Trnavarta thought for a moment. But he did not slow his upwards motion even while thinking. Krishna felt the island continue to rise at the same alarming speed. He glanced down. They were at least a kilometre off the ground and still shooting up fast.

Trnavarta sensed him looking down with his inner eye and a crafty look came into the demon's eyes.

What's the matter, Haridev? Do you fear being so high above the ground? Are you anxious about your mortal body falling to its death?

Krishna smiled.

I told you. I do not care about that mortal form. It is merely a vessel. I can find another.

Trnavarta grinned, his teeth smearing away to particles that turned grey and joined the slipstream flowing downwards.

Even so, great one, I think it might be best if I took us higher.

Krishna felt a surge of power as the island was lifted by a great burst of energy. He saw Trnavarta's form dissolve further as the demon exerted more of his power to propel them skywards. Glancing down, he saw that they were already at least two kilometres above ground and rising at a much faster rate. The yards sped by at a blurring pace. Three kilometres, then four, then five …

Too fast for you, little god-child?

Not at all. But since you do not seem interested in your own survival, I might as well kill you and be done with it.

Krishna lolled his head against the sala tree, deliberately striking it hard. The tree cracked resoundingly, the trunk splitting free of the base. So great was their upward momentum and the resultant force of gravity now that the broken tree tumbled over and over and vanished into the current of the demon's whirlwind. The force of its passage caused the entire island to shudder and wobble dangerously.

Trnavarta looked puzzled and irritated.

What are you doing?

I told you. I do not care about that body's survival. I mean to kill you now.

I do not understand, the demon said. How can you kill me?

By tricking you into carrying us upwards.

Trnavarta stared at him.

What does that mean? It was *I* who lifted you into the air! So that I could drop your body down from a height and kill you.

So you thought. But I was the one who tricked you into doing so. That was why I made my body too heavy for you to pick up, forcing you to raise a whole patch of earth around me, causing you to carry us up at a great speed. Then I tricked you into going even faster, until ...

Until? asked the demon, his wind-swept voice both mournful and doubtful.

Until your momentum was so great, you would be unable to stop yourself even if you wished to.

Krishna glanced around.

As is the case now.

He gestured.

Trnavarta looked around.

They were yojanas up in the sky now. Except that it was no longer the sky. It was the outskirts of the planet's atmosphere, far beyond the limits of the clouds and the upper reaches of the air, and at the rate they were shooting up, they would leave the earth's orbit soon enough and continue into the vast blackness of open space.

Trnavarta gasped.

And struggled for breath.

Krishna smiled.

You see? You forgot that even a wind demon needs wind in order to survive. And wind is only possible where there is air. This high, there is barely air to breathe, let alone blow around, and soon we will leave the motherly grasp of prithviloka and fly out into the directionless emptiness of space.

Trnavarta exerted himself. Krishna watched as the demon's dissipated particles began to collect, cohering into a recognizable whole again. In a moment, he was almost wholly solid, only his lower body and feet still a mass of swirling particles.

I cannot stop us! It is as if I have no more control over our movement!

Krishna smiled again. *That is because wind has no power here. The force of our momentum will continue to carry us forward indefinitely now. We cannot stop. We could travel for crores of years and we would still not come to a halt. Because to stop requires wind resistance or ground friction, and in open space we shall encounter neither. Of course, we may strike another planet or heavenly body and that would halt our progress. But I wouldn't worry about that. You will be dead long before that – you are already gasping for breath, choking in the absence of air. All living creatures need air to breathe, and as a wind demon it is the very blood in your veins. You need more of it to exist.*

Trnavarta began to gasp and choke. He reached out to Krishna beseechingly.

Save me!

Save you? Krishna chuckled. *You came to kill me. Why should I save you?*

I shall serve you forever, Lord! Forgive my transgression. I know your true power now. Spare my life.

Krishna pretended to think a moment. *There is only one way you may be free.*

Anything!

Look into my mouth.

Trnavarta stared at him, then realized he was serious. The demon nodded vigorously and started forward. As his body had solidified, he had drifted downwards to land on the ground. Now, his body fully formed, he strode forward to the spot where little Krishna sat at the foot of the broken tree. He bent down, hesitated, then leaned forward uncertainly.

Krishna opened his mouth wide and showed him the same thing that Yashoda had seen only a short while earlier, before she had set him down under the same tree.

Trnavarta stared, fascinated.

My Lord! I see ...

What do you see?

Trnavarta hesitated.

I see everything. The world, the planets, the movements of the celestial orbs ... it is magnificent. You are magnificent, Lord. You are everything and everything is contained within you.

Krishna pointed upwards. Their movement had slowed now and they were drifting like a raft upon a motionless lake in the cold darkness of space. Krishna could not breathe there and neither could Trnavarta. They would die of air deprivation in moments. But the demon was too overwhelmed by what he had glimpsed to care any more. His eyes reflected his sudden adoration.

Now look up. Tell me what you see.

Trnavarta looked up, out into the vastness of space.

I see ... the same thing I saw within you, Lord! The world, the planets, the movements of the celestial orbs ... it is exactly the same!

And what else do you see? Beyond that?

Trnavarta craned his neck, his breath hitching now, his chest straining for air.

I see ... you, my Lord! Your teeth, your lips, your throat, your tongue ... all that heavenly beauty is contained within your mouth. You bear the universe within yourself. There is proof! I can see it with ... with ... my own eyes ...

Trnavarta fell to the ground, clutching his chest, gasping. He reached out and caught hold of Krishna's left foot, then pulled himself closer until his forehead touched the sole of the baby foot.

Lord ...

Krishna reached out and touched Trnavarta's forehead. The asura gasped one final breath, then released a long plaintive sigh. Motes of his being drifted out of his mouth, floating away into space. This time, they would not return to rejoin the rest of his body. The wind had been taken out of the wind demon.

Krishna looked around. The island of uprooted earth had travelled far beyond the earth's affectionate pull. It was now floating out into the ether. Soon, it would be out among the other planets and then it would travel to the distant stars.

Krishna's physical body required air. And air was in short supply here. He had to return to earth, to the comforting pull of Prithvi Maa and her warm embrace of life-giving air.

He puffed his chubby cheeks and blew slowly. He had to be very careful, for the air in his lungs was the only air left. Once it was gone, he would have no other recourse.

He blew harder, feeling the forward momentum of the island slow, then stop. Harder now. And the island was beginning to move slowly in the opposite direction. Back towards mother earth.

Faster now. Blowing harder. Travelling faster. Blowing fast and furious. Moving at great speed.

And then, that was it. The breath in his lungs was gone. His chest heaved, seeking air desperately.

He glanced back. He could see himself hurtling back towards the planet of his birth, picking up speed.

He gasped as the first vestiges of air began to enter his lungs again. There was barely enough to breathe but it was enough, just enough. He sucked it in greedily.

The edges of the island began to shimmer, then blaze as the speed and intensity of its re-entry caused great friction. The leaves of the trees on the island caught fire, next the grass blazed up around him, then every last bush and creeper and vine and tree trunk went up in flames.

Time to leave this place!

He stood, taking an instant to balance his clumsy pudgy body, then bent and leapt upwards. Upwards and away.

He flew through the air, propelled not by any force or power but by the pull of Prithvi Maa alone. Wind, blessed wind, blew across his face. He plummeted down towards earth. The island fell on its own, turning over and over itself, breaking into pieces and clods and burning wisps. The body of the dead asura fell with it.

Krishna descended upon the earth.

sixteen

The crowd favoured its own men, naturally. The roar of approval that met Crooked Jaw and his team as the members took their positions was deafening. Kamsa glanced around the stadium. There were a thousand score soldiers and more assembled there that night, most of them drunk and battle-fogged from the day's fighting. He had seen similar events often before, but never on this scale. All armies needed some way to release the day's frustrations and pain. But what Jarasandha had done here was unprecedented. He had sponsored the biggest mass entertainment ever heard of, and by centring it around a game involving war stratagem with their own champions, he had made it personal and involving for the men. This had to be the highlight of the day for the men gathered, those who had survived the day's fighting anyway. He saw any number of men exchanging coins in substantial quantities and understood that betting was not only permitted, it was being encouraged. Of course! Jarasandha would be managing the betting and profiting from it as well. He was the 'house', so to speak. And as Kamsa knew well, whether you won or lost, the house always won. Leave it to Jarasandha to find a way to not only boost morale and relieve tension but also profit from it! The consummate multi-caster, merchant and warrior and king and priest, all rolled into one.

Kamsa took stock of his own teammates. They were tough-looking men, of a tribe he had never encountered before nor heard of. From the looks of it, they appeared to be the reserved, reticent type, not saying much, not displaying much emotion, but strong and confident. They exchanged looks, gestures and little touches amongst one another that suggested they had a strong bond. Clearly, they had played before as a team. Jarasandha might take pleasure in humiliating him as well as in winning, but he was not foolish enough to give Kamsa a useless team. The only point of this sport was for both teams to be evenly matched. Otherwise, it would be a very quick and boring game.

He turned to his teammates, drawing their attention. They regarded him dispassionately, neither displaying subservience nor arrogance. They had understood their condition but not accepted it, he saw. They had something to fight for and were willing to do what they had to, even risk their lives, but not kowtow to the enemy or bow and scrape. That pleased him. He respected enemies who chose to lose their necks in battle rather than bend them at someone's feet. He could work with this team; he only needed to be certain that they would accept him and work with him as well.

'I am here to win,' he told them. He used elaborate hand gestures to emphasize his words. 'If we work together, we will surely succeed.'

Then he clenched his fist and pointed it at the sky: 'To victory!'

After a brief pause in which they glanced at one another, they raised their clenched fists as well. 'To victory!' they said in their dialect. He was relieved to note that he knew the dialect. It would make communication easier.

Kamsa heard a commotion in the stadium and looked around. He saw two familiar female shapes entering the royal pavilion above the playing field. His wives, Jarasandha's daughters. They were dressed in rich robes and bejewelled as queens, and looked as coquettish and alluring as ever. They waved excitedly to Kamsa, calling out his name. He nodded, embarrassed, and saw Jarasandha smile down at him. So, his wonderfully considerate father-in-law had decided to add another level of pressure: the prospect of abject humiliation and embarrassment should he lose. It was one thing to lose in front of twenty thousand soldiers; it was unacceptable to do so before one's own wives. For Kamsa, at least.

Which was why he would not lose.

He took his position at the fore centre of his team's playing area, awaiting the signal to begin the game. Bending over, patting his oiled thighs, he recalled the words of Yadu the night before: 'Until now, whatever you did was your own madness. I desire no part in that. But the road you are set on now will lead Mathura to fall into the hands of the Magadhan empire and that I will not tolerate. You may not realize this but Jarasandha desires nothing more than to make the Yadava nation a part of his greater domain.'

'I realize that,' Kamsa had replied, 'and I will not let it happen.'

Yadu scoffed. 'It will happen no matter what you do here. The only way to prevent it is to convince Jarasandha that he is better off letting you run Mathura for him than for him to take over its running. He has enough on his field already to manage. There comes a point when an emperor has to delegate and trust his kings to rule their individual kingdoms. Right now, Jarasandha is not fully convinced that you are capable of doing so. Your record has been ... spotty ... to say the least. But you can prove that you have changed. You can give him confidence in your abilities to manage on your own and keep him at bay.'

'How?' Kamsa asked, genuinely interested. It was a question he asked himself every day. He had known that the last time he had spoken with Jarasandha, he had only bought himself time. Jarasandha had to return to address other issues of secession and rebellion. But sooner or later, he would turn his attention back to Mathura. And if he was not satisfied with how Kamsa was running things, he would wrest it away in a trice, installing his own satrapy and relegating Kamsa once more to the position of a mere puppet figurehead. Kamsa remembered what it had felt like to be such a figurehead, with Bahuka calling the shots, and would never accept such an arrangement again. Yet the only response he could come up with was to use violence, to fight Jarasandha or his champions and prove his ability through superior strength. And that had a certain disadvantage: in an actual fight, no matter how powerful Kamsa might be, Jarasandha was almost certainly stronger, and he had many more champions to spare. There was a limit to how many warriors Kamsa could fight and kill.

'By gaining the respect of your people again,' Yadu said. 'You have done bad things, terrible things that can never be forgotten or forgiven. But you are a warrior and warriors do terrible things. Violence is the wrong path and yet a Kshatriya has no choice but to walk that path all the way to the end, so that other varnas can live their lives peaceably. This is your dharma. But the least you can do is balance the scales. Prove to your people that you do what you do for the betterment of Mathura, for the future of the Yadavas. Put the marauding and madness behind you. You have already suppressed your rakshasa side admirably, that is why I decided it was worthwhile speaking with you. Now, you must rebuild the reputation you have lost and become the king Mathura needs once more.'

Kamsa had only stared at his purported ancestor. It was as if Yadu had stated his entire life goal in words. There was nothing the old man had said that he did not agree with. He had put his rakshasa side behind him; he had turned his back on the madness and marauding. That was the old Kamsa. This Kamsa, the Kamsa he was now, desired to be a king in the true sense of the word. To command dignity, respect, adulation. Even the respect of his own father-in-law. He craved desperately for Jarasandha to acknowledge him as a good king and an equal, not merely a protégé and son-in-law. But how could he achieve such things?

'How?' he had asked.

The old man had smiled, his thousand-wrinkle face creasing like a crumpled leather map that had been folded and refolded too many times. 'By winning.'

Kamsa returned to the present moment, to the stadium in Jarasandha's war camp, where he stood with nineteen other team members, awaiting the signal for the game to begin. Out of the corner of his eye, he saw Jarasandha raise his hand, assenting. Below, the game referee blew a long sharp burst on his carved-bone horn, indicating the start of the game.

The two team captains stepped forward. Kamsa and Crooked Jaw faced each other across the line that separated their two 'kingdoms'. Crooked Jaw glared down at him. 'We will tear you apart limb from limb.'

Kamsa grinned at him. Crooked Jaw had been expecting like threats and bombastic claims from Kamsa, not a congenial smile. He frowned, confused. Kamsa added to his confusion by dropping one eyelid in a mocking wink. Crooked Jaw snarled and shook his fist, almost striking the referee.

Eager for the game to begin, the man in question shouted to be heard above the hubbub of the spectators.

'God Emperor Jarasandha has declared that there will be no restrictions on body blows and strikes. All moves are acceptable. However, there will be no replacements either. If you lose a man, you play with what you have left. The last team standing wins! Jarasandha has also declared that since the Magadhan team won its last match, it has the honour of starting today.'

And with that he stepped back hurriedly, eager to be out of the reach of the two opponents, and blew a sharp short burst on his bone horn.

Choosing to send himself into the fray as the first invader, Crooked Jaw leapt across the line.

The game was on.

seventeen

Yashoda had not stopped crying since the moment she saw the wind demon carry her Krishna up in the sky. To her horror, the demon had uprooted the entire tree along with a large patch of ground on which the tree grew, and carried the whole up high. As she watched, the swirling whirlwind had carried the island of soil and trees up, rising swifter than a chariot, until it was barely a speck in the sky. She ran towards the spot from whence it had risen, collapsed to the ground, and stared up after it until it was lost to sight.

'Krishna!' she cried.

Attempting to comfort his distressed wife, Nanda kept his arm around her. But she knew that his heart was in fragments too. He was crying as copiously as she. For what could he do? What could any parent do to save his or her child from a calamity such as *this*? From a demon who came in the form of a whirlwind and who could uproot entire islands of earth and carry them up into the sky? It was beyond imagining.

'Where has he taken our child?' she asked Nanda, clutching his arms in desperation.

His handsome face, tear-streaked and crumpled with pain, offered no answer.

In time, the other gopis and gopas joined them as well. A great crowd – virtually all of Vrajbhoomi – gathered at the spot of the abduction. For, ever since the incident with Putana, the whole region had been ablaze with rumours of child attacks and abductions. Now, the worst fears had come true. Krishna had been spirited by another rakshasa. More people kept arriving as the word spread. Everyone was agitated, upset, even angry.

'We must join the rebellion,' some said.

'Yes, this is all the Usurper's doing. He is a rakshasa himself and has recruited other demons to kill our little ones.'

'He fears the prophecy of the Slayer, despite the purges of the newborns.'

'Who is to say he will not order another massacre, this time of little children.'

'Or of all children!'

'The only way to fight him is to join the rebellion, go into exile and take up arms against Mathura.'

'Akrur was right. We should ally with the Bhojas and seek King Kuntibhoja's military aid. Together, we can march on Mathura and dethrone the Usurper.'

Tempers grew hotter and the suggestions bolder, more violent.

Nanda listened to all this for some time, then, finally, rose, turning his tear-stained face to the crowd. The men and women broke off their angry chatter and fell quiet at once.

Nanda wiped his face with his sleeve. 'I understand your anger. I have felt it too. But the day Yadavas go to war against Yadavas is a day I do not wish to live to see.'

Some of the softer elements, those who realized the shame and horror of a civil war, asked gently, 'What would you have us do, then, Nanda Maharaja? Things cannot go on as they have until today.'

Nanda nodded slowly. 'I know this better than you. I am the one who has lost his son today.'

Everyone nodded and agreed with him. He had more right to speak than they did.

'Yet the solution to violence is not more violence. The answer to oppression is not rebellion, nor is war an answer to any problem.'

The harder elements, those who advocated rebellion and civil war on a daily basis, were ruffled by this answer. While retaining a show of respect for their dearly loved chieftain, they asked gruffly, 'What is the solution, then? Shall we stand by and do nothing as our children are slaughtered?'

Nanda looked this last speaker directly in the eye. While a man of peace to the core, Nanda was not a weak man. Like all those who choose the path of non-violence, he was, if anything, stronger than most warriors. For, though any fool can take up a sword and shake it, it takes a truly brave man to refuse to pick up a sword when one is already pointing at your throat. 'The solution has already been given to us. Have you forgotten what Gargamuni told us? What all the elders and wise men have told us?'

Everyone nodded. 'The Slayer!' they said aloud in unison.

'Aye,' Nanda went on. 'The Slayer. He has been born. And he got away from under Kamsa's nose despite his best attempts. That itself is proof enough of his power. The day is not far when he will rise and rid the earth of the blasphemy that is the Usurper. And then we shall all be free. And we shall have achieved that freedom without fighting our brothers in Mathura, or pitting half our nation against the other half in a bloody civil war that may go on long after Kamsa himself is gone.'

There was wisdom in his words and even the most hard-line political radicals in the gathering sensed and acknowledged it. Some still felt that immediate action was needed. After all, they argued, if the Slayer was only recently born, it would surely take a great many years before he grew old and strong enough to face a being as formidable as the Usurper. How were they to survive until then?

'By migrating out of Vraj,' Nanda said.

This announcement sent shock ripples through the gathering. 'Migrate? You mean exile? Leave our land? Our nation? Our herds?'

Everyone knew what had happened to Akrur and the other chieftains who had led the exodus to Bhoja and other neighbouring kingdoms: their lands and herds had been annexed on the Usurper's orders and they had lost everything. They lived now as permanent exiles, condemned to execution on sight if caught. It was not a life most desired. The hardliners were silent and grim, feeling that exile was better than living in humiliation, but they still could not see how this was in line with Nanda's desire to wait until the Slayer arose to do his task.

Nanda set their doubts at rest. He shook his head. 'Nay. Nothing as drastic as exile. We shall not leave this beautiful god-given earth. We shall merely move to a nearby location, a place where the Usurper's soldiers will not find us easily and where we can bide our time until the Slayer rises.'

'Where?' they clamoured. But some already knew, for Nanda had been discussing this very option for weeks now, ever since the first attempt on Krishna's life. They had even helped make secret arrangements. But now they waited for Nanda to reveal his plans in his own words.

'Vrindavan,' Nanda said.

'The forest? Among the wild creatures?' some asked, alarmed. It sounded almost as bad as going into exile. Filled with unknown predators, Vrindavan was a large and dark forest. And being big enough to lose one's way, it was not anyone's idea of a good place to live.

'There is a secret grove within the forest,' Nanda said. 'It was set off a long time ago in order to breed different varieties of honeybees to produce the famous honey from which the soma, honey wine, is prepared. Its location is a secret to all but a certain section of wine makers, because they did not wish for anyone else to have access to that special honeybee and its heavenly produce. It is large enough for us to live comfortably, a small Vrajbhoomi within the heart of the great forest. It can be accessed via a secret pathway from the gardens. My friend Vasudeva told me of its location and suggested that if things became too difficult here, we could seek shelter there.'

'Can we take our herds there?' someone asked hopefully. For most Vrishnis, exile was less terrible than leaving one's herds behind.

'Yes,' Nanda said. 'We can rebuild our houses there and live as comfortably as we do here. However, we shall have to be careful with our cook fires to avoid giving away the secret location. But if we post watches at strategic locations and do not venture out from there, it will be nigh impossible for the Usurper's soldiers to find us. They are more likely to lose themselves in the forest than stumble across this secret nook.'

Everyone looked at one another. There seemed to be no real objection to this plan. Even the hardliners, disgruntled as they were about the lack of violent response, admitted to themselves that for the time being, waiting and watching was the wiser option.

There was only one question that troubled everyone.

'What if the Slayer never rises?' asked a lone voice of doubt.

Nanda sighed and looked at Yashoda. She had stopped weeping only because she had been drained of tears. But she was still watching the sky and praying silently, unwilling to lose hope.

'I believe the prophecy. The Slayer will come,' he said.

'And what if he fails?'

Nanda was silent. He did not know how to answer that.

Just then, Yashoda started forward. 'Look,' she said hoarsely, her throat choked with too much crying. 'Look!' she said louder, pointing upwards.

Everyone turned their attention skywards, peering up.

Even Nanda looked up, curious.

He saw it.

A speck, growing larger as it approached very, very quickly. Now it was a tiny dot, then a larger dot, then it was the size of a little fingertip, and later the size of a thumb ... and it was growing larger quite fast.

'Krishna!' Nanda heard himself say.

eighteen

C rooked Jaw lunged forward in an attacking move. Kamsa's teammates were spread out in a semicircle surrounding the intruder, blocking his way, ready to grasp hold of him if he tried to make a rush at their 'home' line, but also wary of coming within his clutches. His goal was to try to reach their home line while theirs was to stop him from doing so. It was basic war strategy: the enemy attempted to take one's prime city, your army attempted to stop him.

The game required the intruder to constantly chant a single word. It could be anything the player or team wished, so long as it was chanted constantly, without pause. The effect was to prevent the intruder from drawing breath too easily and to make him tire much faster, thereby pressuring him to either achieve the enemy's home line or 'perish'. The Magadhan team's word was, predictably, 'Magadha' and Crooked Jaw repeated it over and over again, 'Magadha Magadha Magadha Magadha …' as he feinted this way, then that. Among other things, the referee's task was to ensure that all players chanted their word without pause or respite, failing which they would be deemed to have perished and be removed to the sidelines.

Crooked Jaw's chest was a huge barrel, which was probably the reason why the giant could continue his feinting and chanting without tiring for several moments. The crowd kept cheering him on, certain of its team's victory. Kamsa assumed that the home team almost always won these games, because if it lost, even if some of the players survived the game itself, they would not survive Jarasandha's disapproval afterwards. That was strong motivation to win and it showed on the larger man's face as he danced with surprising agility from one end of the field to the other, sending Kamsa's teammates rippling this way, then that, in order to maintain a solid wall.

Finally, Crooked Jaw made his move. Feinting right, he lunged left, then dodged the other way, waited till Kamsa's teammates rushed to block that side, then turned around and ran the same way but got past the first wall of players.

Attempting to knock him off his feet, the player he had successfully dodged made the mistake of lunging at him and grabbing his torso with both hands.

It was a serious mistake.

Once a player made contact, the intruder was free to use whatever force necessary to free himself. Other players could join in, but if the intruder then crossed the line of the area they were guarding, they would be out of the game instantly. The player who attacked Crooked Jaw had to either stop him now or forfeit his own part in the game.

But that was the least of his problems.

Crooked Jaw roared with delight, pleased rather than angry, and he shouted his muttered chant to express his pleasure. 'Magadha Magadha Magadha!' he chanted loudly. And the crowd, smelling first blood, roared in response: 'MAGADHA! MAGADHA! MAGADHA!'

Kamsa's teammate held his grip around Crooked Jaw's torso. Crooked Jaw raised his elbow and brought it down on the other man's back in a stabbing motion. Now, with ordinary men, this would hurt the man a little, depending on how much muscle and self-discipline he had accumulated. But with the special powers Crooked Jaw possessed, the effect was devastating.

The elbow struck the man's back and broke through it. Blood spattered in a great splash, falling on the dusty ground in globules. Crooked Jaw's elbow pierced the man's backbone, ribs and lungs, and exposed his entire inner workings. He screamed as the last breath left his lungs and Crooked Jaw tossed him to the ground like a sack of yams. The man fell and lay bleeding, his ribcage and chest a shattered mess, already dead.

That was why Magadha's team always won: each player was empowered by Jarasandha through the use of his special potions which he had designed after he had seen the unexpected effect they had had on his son-in-law. Kamsa had thought himself to be the only one possessed of such an ability, but clearly that was no longer the case, if it had ever been. Jarasandha had found a way to create more men with the same ability, and logically, if the man was bigger and stronger and tougher to begin with, the more formidable he would be after empowerment. Like Crooked Jaw. Or the rest of his teammates, all of whom were taller and wider and apparently stronger than Kamsa.

On the other hand, the other teams were ordinary mortal men, with all the weaknesses that normal mortal flesh was subject to. Like the man with the shattered chest who lay at Crooked Jaw's feet now.

Crooked Jaw turned and flashed Kamsa a smile before turning and crossing to the second block.

For the first time, Kamsa's teammates were agitated. Whatever they had thought or heard of the Magadhans, they had not been prepared for this. They had assumed even the earlier demonstration with the sword to be some kind of trickery done with a wooden sword. Now, they were coming to terms with the realization that it had been real, that these were men whose skin was tough enough to resist the sharpest blade and who were possessed of greater strength than any normal man, and it was too much. They screamed at each other and cried out, unsure what to do.

'Hold the line!' Kamsa shouted over their cries.

They ignored him.

'HOLD! THE! LINE!' he yelled, louder this time.

They heard him this time, but looked at him as if he were insane.

But those on the second row understood and did as he bid. They held their line, blocking Crooked Jaw's way.

Perhaps they thought that despite his superior strength and ability, they might still block him by skill. The game was played with variations everywhere, Kamsa knew, and every soldier who played it took pride in his skill. The best champions of the sport were often celebrated and famous in their armies and admired by all.

Kamsa shouted instructions to his mates as Crooked Jaw continued his muttered chant, dodging the second wall of defenders now, seeking a way to dodge past them without making physical contact. Again, as was obvious, it was not that the intruder feared the contact itself but that he feared being disqualified.

Again, he dodged and feinted and dodged again. But this time the players followed Kamsa's instructions and simply held their positions, not moving an inch. Nobody responded to Crooked Jaw's feints and dodges and after several tries the giant grew frustrated.

'Magadha!' he cried and charged headlong at the space between two of his opponents. He meant to barrel through them and run all the way to the home line, Kamsa knew. And with his superior size and ability, he would be able to achieve just that. And any of Kamsa's players who touched him to try to stop him would be taken out of the game, one way or another. Kamsa was expecting that; it was the reason he had ordered the second line to stay still and force the Magadhan's hand.

Now, he leapt at the Magadhan himself. Even though he was front and centre, there was nothing to stop him from going after an intruder from behind, except the fact that if the intruder crossed the second line while still in contact with Kamsa, Kamsa would be disqualified from the game.

But Kamsa had no intention of letting him reach the second line. He began running the instant Crooked Jaw began moving forward. Lighter on his feet, he was able to move much faster than the larger, heavier man, and he was not burdened with having to chant a word constantly and deplete his breath. He pounded in an arc, sprinting at an angle that brought him in direct contact with Crooked Jaw, and slammed into the Magadhan's right side, taking him completely by surprise. Had any of his teammates attempted this same manoeuvre, the result would have been akin to a child running into the side of an elephant. But Kamsa had hardened his body density to the maximum possible and he was as heavy and tough as granite itself. He struck the Magadhan with enough force to rattle him and throw him off his forward momentum. Once Crooked Jaw was turned aside, his own running force carried him the rest of the way.

Crooked Jaw fell and tumbled, rolling over once before coming to a halt with a heavy thud. Kamsa felt the impact of the thud – it was far heavier than the impact of his own shoulder hitting the ground. Kamsa looked up and checked his position: he had fallen safe, within the chalk line of his *kingdom's* boundary.

Crooked Jaw, on the other hand, had fallen just over the line, which meant that he would have to go to the sidelines and wait until one of his teammates crossed to the home line and brought him back into the game.

The bone horn blew a short, sharp burst, indicating that Crooked Jaw was out for the moment and the referee pointed to the sideline. Crooked Jaw glared at the referee as if he would like to wring his neck, but he rose to his feet and went quietly to the sideline. But he did so after glaring pointedly at Kamsa.

Kamsa grinned. If he wanted, Crooked Jaw could demolish the entire enemy team single-handedly in a moment. He demolished scores of them each day during battle. But this was different. This was a sport and there were rules and tens of thousands of his admirers watching. He would want to win within the bounds of the rules, not by breaking them. That was what Kamsa had counted on, and which Yadu had reminded him of. 'The limitations that you find frustrating are also your greatest assets. Use them against your opponent. In war, as in sport, the goal is the same. Use what you are given in unexpected yet effective ways. He who does so most shrewdly wins on both fields.' That was what the old man had taught him the night before: how to win at this game. For he had known that Jarasandha would send for Kamsa soon and that he would use this very game to try to humiliate and undermine him as a precursor to justifying taking control of Mathura. How Yadu had known this, Kamsa did not know. It hardly mattered. But he understood that the forebear of the Yadava race could only have the interests of the Yadavas at heart, and, eager to learn as much as he could in those short hours, he had listened and trained intently all night. It helped that he had played the same game often before as a boy and a youth – although in a much milder form without such violence – and that he had actually been quite good at it.

Now he grinned at Crooked Jaw, savouring his first victory of the game.

Kamsa's teammates were ecstatic but reserved.

'He is out for now,' they said to Kamsa. 'But when he returns …?'

'And what of his teammates?' asked another troubled voice. 'If they are all as invulnerable as he is, what chance do we have?'

Kamsa smiled. 'We take the battle to them.'

Then he turned to the referee and indicated himself. The referee nodded and came forward to point at Kamsa, blowing his horn again to indicate that the captain of the enemy team was now using his turn to send himself into the Magadhan domain.

Kamsa glanced up. Jarasandha was watching with a deceptively genial expression. His daughters waved excitedly, pleased to see their husband achieve his first moment of victory.

Perhaps after I win this game, I will go to them tonight, Kamsa thought. *In their father's own tent.* He grinned at the prospect and leapt forward into the enemy quadrant, slapping his thighs and chanting the word he had chosen as his team's mantra. 'Mathura Mathura Mathura …' he chanted as he moved into enemy territory.

nineteen

Shouts went up from the Vrishnis as they saw the falling object burst into flames. Many screamed in horror as it then broke into pieces and the individual burning fragments plummeted downwards. Nanda had put his arm around Yashoda again and clutched her tightly as they stared skywards. She gasped and screamed when the fragments began to break up further into smaller bits and pieces. Some were all fire and ash long before they reached the earth. How could any living creature survive either the fire or the fall?

Then the pieces began to fall. The Vrishnis screamed and some began running in panic. But Nanda shouted to them to hold still. If they were hit, so be it. As he saw it, they stood a better chance of survival by staying in one place – that way the objects might not fall upon them directly.

His judgement proved correct.

The fragments of the flaming object began to crash down to earth over the hill, well away from where they had gathered. The rise protected them from any debris flung up or shards that might have been sent flying from the various impacts.

When everything had finished falling, Nanda gave his clansmen leave to go and inspect.

The whole gathering proceeded up the hill.

Yashoda realized that she no longer felt weighed down by leaden feet. She could practically sprint up the hill now, energized by her desire to see if her Krishna had somehow, miraculously, survived the fall. She could not believe he could be dead.

The sight from the top of the hill was shocking.

Debris lay spread across the rolling valley. The decorations and arrangements for the festivities were destroyed or in flames but nobody cared about that. Chunks of tree trunks, clods of earth, rocks and boulders were strewn all over.

The crowd spread out, searching among the fallen debris for any signs of life.

The Vrishnis came across the corpse of Trnavarta first. A great hue and cry rose up. Nanda and Yashoda moved through the crowd that had already gathered to view the asura's ghastly remains.

His body had been all but burnt to ashes by the fire and lay sprawled across a great boulder. It was impossible to say whether it was the fall that had killed him or the flames. Either way, there was no doubt that he was dead.

Yashoda wanted to spit on the corpse and curse the demon for having abducted her son. But seeing him dead like that, she held back her anger, knowing it would achieve nothing.

She turned and walked away. Most of the Vrishnis still crowded around the rakshasa's body, awed. Most had never seen an asura until Putana's death. This made it two. They could hardly believe that these creatures of folklore and legend actually existed and moved about them in human form. Who knew in what form the next one might come?

Her mind harried by the sight of the dead asura, Yashoda wandered away. If the attacker himself was dead, what hope could there be for her little one? After falling from such a height …?

Maatr, why do you worry so? I told you, no harm will ever befall me. I am your son, after all. I have drunk your milk, and that makes me extra-special!

'Krishna!' she cried, spinning around.

Nanda came to her.

'Where are you, Krishna?' she cried.

Nanda took hold of Yashoda's hand. 'Beloved one, even if his body lies here, perhaps it would be best if you do not look upon it in this condition …'

'Krishna!' she cried out. To Nanda she said distractedly: 'He is alive, Nanda. He just spoke to me!'

Nanda blinked.

I am here, Maatr. On the patch of grass, sitting and waiting.

Yashoda swung around. There, over by the marigolds, she saw him now. A little chubby form sitting on his buttocks, waving and smiling.

'Krishna, my son!' she cried and ran to him. Nanda followed her, bewildered at first, then with a shout of excitement as he too spotted Krishna. The others heard their cries and left the asura's body to come running.

Krishna was getting to his feet just as Yashoda reached him. He raised his hands to her happily. 'Maa,' he cried.

'Krishna!' she said, picking him up and hugging him harder than she had ever hugged him before. 'Oh my son! I knew you were safe and well. I knew it!'

Nanda came up and hugged his wife and son, kissing little Krishna on the forehead. 'You are well! It is a miracle. It is God's grace.'

The Vrishnis crowded around them, excited and happy, and though none of them had actually done anything, they began cheering and congratulating one another. They were all ecstatically happy that their little Krishna was alive and well.

'Vishnu has protected him once again,' they cried out to each other. 'Our prayers and rituals of protection worked brilliantly. He was saved from the second attack as well!'

Cheering, they returned with Nanda and Yashoda to Vrajbhoomi where they celebrated Krishna's survival for the second time. Some of the gopas and gopis took care of the asura's remains, doing as they had done with Putana – chopping the body to pieces and burning it again, until it had turned to ash. Again, they noted how sweet-smelling the smoke from his pyre was, just like the smoke from Putana's. 'He died blessed because he was slain by Vishnu's hand,' they said to one another, not knowing how accurate they actually were.

Back home, Yashoda felt great elation. Her anxiety of the weeks before had vanished. She knew now that Krishna would endure and survive whatever befell him. She wished there would be no more attacks but knew that her son had a great destiny and that her wishing things to be different would not make it so. What mattered was that he would not come to harm, no matter what his enemies did. She believed that now.

Nanda was relieved too. He was accosted by Gargamuni who arrived when the celebrations were well under way.

'Gurudev,' Nanda said, performing the ritual greetings with great joy. 'It is an honour to receive you on this special day. Once again, Lord Vishnu has chosen to grace our son with his blessings. Haridev himself has protected our Krishna.'

Gargacharya glanced at Yashoda and little Krishna across the room on the other cot, and at little Balarama sitting on Rohini's knee nearby, and said to Nanda: 'Good Nanda, you are right. Haridev himself has graced and protected your son. Because your Krishna is none other than Vishnu incarnate himself.'

Nanda stared at the guru.

Garga nodded. 'What I say is true, Nanda Maharaja. Your little Krishna is the Slayer of Narada's prophecy. He was birthed by your friend Vasudeva and Devaki when under imprisonment in Kamsa's palace. Vasudeva spirited him away from Mathura and brought him here the very night of his birth and exchanged him for your newly born daughter. She in turn was Yogamaya herself, who took birth in order to help Vishnu in this mission. She did not die at Kamsa's hands but escaped and returned to swargaloka. All this was done so that Kamsa would not find out that Devaki's eighth child is still alive and well and living in your house as your son. It was essential that you believe he was your son in order for the secret to remain under wraps. Now that you have seen him defeat two powerful asuras, there can be no doubt in your mind of his power, even as an infant. Imagine the great power he shall wield when he is grown to manhood? Rejoice, Nanda, Haridev himself chose to be raised as your son in your house. What greater privilege can a Vishnu-bhakt like you desire?'

Nanda was stunned by this news but recovered quickly. A part of him had always known something was unique about his little dark wonder. And today when he saw Krishna survive that great fall from the sky, he had no doubts left. He accepted every word his guru said.

'It is true,' he said. 'I am greatly blessed.'

'Do not speak of this openly,' Gargamuni warned, 'for there may be more asuras among your people even now, disguised as humans. Only you, Rohini and Yashoda know the truth, for Rohini's son Balarama – Krishna's half-brother – is a partial avatar of Vishnu as well. While not as powerful as your Krishna, he too has a great role to play in the events to come in future years. All that matters now is that you take care of your people and give Balarama and Krishna time to grow to manhood to fulfil the prophecy and then achieve great things on earth.'

Nanda mused over Gargamuni's words. He discussed the matter with Yashoda that night, and took Rohini's suggestions into account as well. The next day, he called a meeting of his family and most trusted Vrishni elders and conferred with them for many long hours.

Finally, they all reached a consensus: the Vrishnis would accept Nanda's suggestion of the day before and plan to migrate to the secret grove of Vrindavan in the event of a calamity. They could stay there safely until the Slayer rose and destroyed the Usurper. They did not worry about the Usurper confiscating their lands – they were confident that when they were away, Vishnu would ensure their homes and lands were kept safe for them. While none but Nanda and his wives knew the truth about who the Slayer was, the rest of the Vrishnis were now convinced that Haridev himself looked over them constantly. They were certain of his protection during their exile in Vrindavan. Finally, it was decided that even if they did not migrate at once, they would ensure that the secret settlement in Vrindavan was ready to house them at a moment's notice so that they could leave at the first sign of trouble.

They began making preparations at once. It would take some time yet, for there was much work to be done and Nanda did not see any need for haste. They also had to be careful to make the move suddenly. It should seem as if the Vrishnis had simply vanished from Vraj one day. They set about planning and preparing for the great migration with the same careful attention and efficiency with which they managed their cows and produced the famous buttermilk, curds and other dairy products that made Vraj renowned the world over.

twenty

Four of them came at him at the same time.

Crooked Jaw's teammates did not have any reason to hold back. They knew what they were capable of, and after enduring the ignominy of watching their captain being sent to the sidelines by Kamsa, they wanted revenge. They were all bigger and tougher than he was, and felt confident that they could destroy him easily, even in a one-on-one combat.

But just to be sure, they came at him together, with the intention to not merely knock him out of the game but to kill him. Kamsa had no way of knowing if this was on Jarasandha's orders or merely their own death wish for him.

They were smart — he had to give them that much — and were experienced warriors, so they didn't come at him from the front, giving him a chance to flail out at them. Two of them came from either side at precisely the same time, forcing him to choose whether to strike out in one direction or the other. The other two attacked him from behind, also at the same time, one going high, the other low. They intended to ram and crush him, breaking his bones and smashing his vital organs.

He stood still and let them try.

They struck him with the combined force of four chariots striking in a head-on collision. Usually, when his body was this hardened, Kamsa felt nothing, merely observed and heard the impact of a boulder he threw or a stone he had crushed, or an iron rod striking his body. He would feel the superficial impact – the vibrations, shuddering, the sound of something thudding against his petrified flesh – but not actually *feel* anything.

But this time, he felt it.

Felt the massive weight of their combined tonnage hitting him. Felt it through his skin as hard as lead sheet, his flesh as rigid as iron, his bones as solid as granite, right to the core of his being. They must have struck him with the combined force of at least a ton of weight, enough to pulverize anything to ruin.

He withstood it.

It was the densest he had ever made his body. He had compacted himself so much that he could feel his heart pumping only once every several seconds, the blood barely trickling through his stony veins. He was almost a block of stone. He had known he could make himself this hard – any of them could, he was sure – but most of the time it was impractical because he needed to move about and so had to keep himself somewhat flexible. The more dense he made his body, the more rigid it became. Right now, he was all but wholly stone, a veritable statue.

They had not been expecting that. They had expected him to move, to lash out, to try and dodge or escape the impact. They had moved fast, in order to strike unexpectedly as well as to coordinate their timing, and hit at exactly the same time. This meant that they had only partially hardened their bodies, more than enough to crush him, but not so much that they could not move or control their limbs.

And instead of them crushing him, he crushed them.

The same force of impact that they inflicted upon him rebounded on them.

It was like hitting a stone wall with an iron fist.

As it turned out, he was the smarter one.

He saw the two who rammed his shoulders break their own. He saw their arms crumple and crack open, like wood split by an axe, and the petrified flesh and blood within exposed like an iced corpse cut open – marbled veins and gelatinous blood. He saw the white of their bones exposed, snapping, breaking, showing jagged edges.

He could not see the ones who struck him from behind, of course. Nor had he felt them strike him. He could feel nothing, actually.

It took him only an instant of concentration to reduce his density enough to enable him to move. And he felt the piercing thirst that always accompanied severe densification at once. He felt like he could drink a barrel or three right then.

Later, he promised himself. *Time enough for food, drink and celebration later.*

He stepped out of the tangle of bodies, turned and examined the results.

All four of his attackers lay on the ground, two with shoulders split open, one with his collarbone shattered into pieces, the fourth with chest and ribcage and lower jaw broken in several places – all the points where their bodies had slammed into his. All because they had sought to rush him fast and he had stood stone still. Literally stone still.

'Mathura Mathura Mathura …'

The words continued from his barely parted lips. It was the only thing he had kept up unceasingly through the scant seconds of the attack.

He looked at the enemy team. The men were staring at him with gaping mouths. Never before had anyone downed four of their teammates at one go. Then again, they had never faced anyone like Kamsa ever before.

He had taken out the entire front line in a single move.

Now he moved across the first border to the second section.

'Mathura Mathura Mathura …'

Kamsa realized that the crowd had gone silent. The utter silence was deafening. The audience had probably been watching these games for years, and was so accustomed to watching its home team win, it probably had no conception that it was even *possible* for its prized warriors to lose.

He would show them it was possible.

The other team members had recovered from the shock of their comrades' failure.

Six of them made a wall across the second quadrant, blocking his way effectively. Two more lurked on the edges, as a backup measure.

None of them made a move to rush him this time. Instead, they watched him warily, stepping this way, then that, to keep the wall tight yet mobile, showing him that they could match any move he made and block him.

Which was what he had expected.

He turned right sharply and sprinted to the side of the quadrant. Because they had all held the line tight to block his way, there was a gap of about three yards at that end. It was unusual for anyone to run fast in the game because of the risk of failing to catch one's breath with the constant chanting. But Kamsa was willing to take that risk. He sprinted right to the side of the quadrant, where the referee stood with his bone horn, saw the look of surprise in the man's eyes – surprise mingled with more than a little fear, for the man had already seen what Kamsa was capable of doing – then swung sharply left, through the gap. The opposing team had guessed what he was up to the instant he started sprinting, and the players on that side had begun moving to block the gap. But they were slower than he was, and only two made it in time.

Kamsa barrelled straight into them, aiming for their arms, which they had made the mistake of linking together in a foolish bid to block him more effectively.

He tore their arms from their sockets. The cracking and ripping sounds of the arms being torn out of the hardened bodies rang loud in the stadium. He threw the torn arms aside and continued his run at the same pace.

'Mathuramathuramathura ...' he chanted non-stop.

There were ten players holding the last quadrant. All of them had begun rushing towards that end of the quadrant the moment he moved that side. But he dodged this way and that as he came, making them unsure of which way he would go. As a result, their line was ragged and each player was separated from the others by a yard or three.

He ran straight at the nearest player and grabbed hold of him. The man was not expecting a direct assault, of all things, but he wasn't wholly unprepared either. He reacted by grasping hold of Kamsa as well. Kamsa had taken hold of the man's head in a vice-like grip and now, as the man struggled, he began to choke him while pushing his head backwards. The man in turn had taken hold of Kamsa's torso and was attempting to crush his softer rear organs on the sides.

Kamsa hardened his body instantly, and shoved with all his strength. The man tried to harden his body but was a fraction of an instant too late. Kamsa heard the sound of the iron-hard neck cracking and saw the Magadhan player's head bend backwards, then topple over till the back of his head touched his upper back. Kamsa let the body drop. It fell with a dull thud to the dust of the ground.

He charged at the next player.

This man too was somewhat surprised at the assault. It was usual for the defending team to attack the intruder, not for the intruder to rush at the defenders!

Also, once body contact was made, the two players had to either wrestle one another to the ground till one yielded, or push one another across the border lines.

Kamsa wrestled the man. He was very wide across, with a thick middle, so Kamsa had gone for his thigh instead. Grasping hold of it, Kamsa threw his own body backwards, knocking both of them off their feet. The man fell backwards, landing heavily on his back. Kamsa had a much lesser distance to fall and was the one doing the throwing, so could land with less impact. Still, it was an effort to keep the chant going and exert pressure on the man's thigh. He climbed atop the man at an angle, grabbing his langot and pulling it to gain a purchase. With ordinary wrestlers, pulling the langot was an effective wrestling move because it exerted pressure on a man's most sensitive parts. But with these men, each part of whose bodies were as strong as iron, it made little difference. What it did achieve was giving Kamsa a handhold.

Using the man's langot to turn around, Kamsa caught hold of the man's arm and then his thigh again.

Then he stood up.

Straining under the weight of the heavier man, he heaved him up like a sack of bricks – or iron ingots, from the feel of him – and flung him across the border line.

The man roared in fury as he realized his mistake too late. But by then he was already thudding down … across the border line and out of the game. Hurling abuses at Kamsa, he slammed his fist on the ground in frustration. He would have got to his feet and run back into the quadrant but for the referee who blew his bone horn at once.

Kamsa turned and saw that the others had no intention of waiting for him to work his wiles on them as well.

Two of them came at him, taking hold of his upper and lower half respectively. Their intention was probably to twist his body in different directions, either tearing him into two pieces, or contorting him hard enough to injure him severely.

Kamsa rolled over the head of the man who was trying to grab his lower half, kicking out at the face of the higher one at the same time.

The move was not sufficient to break him free of their combined grasp but was enough to cause them to lose their balance. As each was pulling in a different direction, they tumbled together, their grip on Kamsa loosening slightly, just enough for him to grasp hold of their arms and twist in opposite directions. He spun like a corkscrew in mid-air, using their hold on his body against them.

Both arms twisted at impossible angles, then were turned like wet rags being wrung out to dry.

The men screamed in pain and shock – even though their bodies were hardened, they were mobile enough to feel such severe trauma. Blood spattered Kamsa from both sides, splashing his chest and back. It was cooler than normal blood, and Kamsa surmised that it was because of the hardening. The more sluggish their bodies became, the slower the flow and the lower the blood temperature.

Kamsa landed on his feet again and turned to the next opponent. He circled three or four of the enemy players as they watched him warily.

By now, Crooked Jaw was yelling orders from the sidelines, frustrated at being out of the game and watching his team being destroyed by a single man.

Kamsa grinned at them, and waved to Crooked Jaw who was even more infuriated and began hurling curses.

'Mathura Mathura Mathura …' Kamsa muttered.

He wrestled his way through the rest of the team. It was hard but satisfying work. Every one of the moves Yadu had shown him came in useful and worked perfectly, including the more complex hand-foot combinations that required considerable agility and effort. It was as if the old Yadava had known precisely how his enemies would attack or respond. He supposed that was true in a sense: there were only so many ways in which a man could wrestle or physically block another man. And of those ways, there were even fewer effective ways to do so in the course of this game.

When at last he crossed the enemy team's home line, the crowd erupted in a huge wave of reluctant admiration and applause. The audience simply could not believe its eyes. Never before had it seen such a thing done, he learnt later. Well, not precisely. They had seen it done only once before, when Crooked Jaw came to play against the Magadhan team before being inducted into it. An enemy chieftain – like all the members of the Magadhan team – he had worked his way through Jarasandha's entire squad of champions just as Kamsa had done today, making mincemeat of them all. It had been even more formidable because Crooked Jaw had not possessed the power to densify his body back then. On the other hand, neither had the Magadhans. This new level of bodily prowess was a relatively recent development.

But Kamsa had faced an entire team of empowered Magadhans and demolished them, and that must surely count as a greater achievement.

As Kamsa raised his clenched fist, surrounded by the ecstatic teammates, all of whom would now be freed along with their tribes, Kamsa saw Crooked Jaw coming towards him, his ugly face dark and furrowed with anger. Kamsa turned to face him, his teammates moving aside to make way for the giant.

Kamsa hardened his body, prepared for any attack. The game was officially over, but he knew that sometimes the real fight began after the game ended. Especially in army camps.

Crooked Jaw stopped a yard short of him. He glared down at Kamsa for a long moment.

'Mathuran!' he roared, making the word sound like an insult.

Kamsa waited.

'You demolished my team!' Crooked Jaw shouted.

Kamsa said nothing.

Crooked Jaw raised a clenched fist.

Kamsa braced himself.

Crooked Jaw raised the other fist, also clenched.

Kamsa waited warily.

Crooked Jaw opened both fists and joined the palms together in a gesture of namaskar. 'I bow to you in grace,' he said gruffly.

Unable to comprehend what had happened, Kamsa stared at him a moment. Then he realized what had happened and felt a surge of laughter bubble up. The giant was acknowledging his victory! It was the highest compliment one sportsman could pay another.

Kamsa clasped the man's joined palms with his own hands. Then he realized that in thinking of his opponent in terms of his deformity, he had forgotten what the warrior had introduced himself as in the arena. If they were about to become friends, he could hardly continue to think of him as Crooked Jaw. And he had a feeling that the man might not take kindly to the name being used aloud either.

'Well met, Warrior. What is your name again?'

'I am Mustika, remember?' said the giant with the crooked jaw. 'And from this day onwards we shall be friends and sporting partners.'

Kamsa grinned. 'So be it.'

Kaand II

Aften the attack of the wind demon and Gargamuni's revelations, Yashoda and Nanda no longer lived in constant anxiety. While as parents they could never truly stop worrying about their child, they no longer worried to the extent that they used to. They knew that no matter what, Krishna would be safe. They had seen proof of that for themselves.

The planning for the migration to Vrindavan also demanded a great deal of their attention and time. And they were also kept busy by the fact that it was the season for calving and many of their cows were due to drop calves any day.

While Yashoda grew busier, Rohini had no pressing demands on her time. So it came to pass that more and more often it was Rohini who sat and watched over Krishna while Yashoda went about her chores. This meant that Krishna and Balarama spent more time together and the boys clearly enjoyed this greatly. They were both at that difficult age where they could walk and were developing their strength and were able to get into mischief more easily. And when it came to mischief, if one was a handful to manage, both together were impossible!

Rohini would take her eyes off them for a moment to attend to something minor and off they would go, crawling about in the dust of Vraj like serpents on an urgent mission. Or they would get to their feet together, holding on to one another's shoulders for support, and start walking arm in arm, like two gopas walking behind their herds.

Once, Rohini realized they were gone but mistook their direction and went the wrong way in search of them. By the time she corrected her error and caught up with the two rascals, they were halfway across a field filled with lowing cows. Somehow, in the course of traversing that field, one of them had accidentally reached out and caught hold of a cow's tail to keep his balance. The cow had lowed loudly in protest and the boys had laughed in merriment, amused at the reaction. Thereafter, they had both taken to going around and tugging every cow tail in sight.

Rohini had completely lost sight of them by then and was going out of her mind trying to guess where they could have vanished so suddenly. She was alerted by the irritated lowing of the cows and peered at the field. Finally, she spotted their chubby shapes moving between the cows' legs, the udders often higher than their little curly haired heads. She cried out in indignation and went running to catch them. Just then, one of them tugged particularly hard at an ageing cow's tail, causing it considerable distress. The half-blind cow took great offence at the prank and, not realizing that it was Haridev himself who had committed the crime, reared back and kicked out hard. Both boys tumbled and rolled over and over on the ground, but their falls were softened by their landing in a large patch of something soft and cushiony. When Rohini came across them, they were both lying together and laughing merrily, covered from head to toe in fresh cow dung.

On another occasion, they both caught hold of a cow's tail together and wanted to pull it. Each insisted he was the first to grab it and so he should be the one to pull it. With neither willing to relinquish hold of the poor cow's appendage, they argued fiercely in their baby talk. Finally, in pain from the constant pulling, the cow began to run, and the brothers still refused to let go.

At the sound of Rohini's and Yashoda's voices, all the women in Vraj came out of their houses and saw Balarama and Krishna being dragged along by a cow who appeared to be trying to win a race in which the boys' mothers – clearly only the runners-up – were yelling to them to let go of the tail!

Their pranks grew bolder. Once, a snake slithered into the compound and was spotted at once by Krishna. He trotted off to examine the new arrival. Rohini saw Krishna from where she sat, but could not see the snake due to a depression in the ground. She assumed he was merely out for a walk and so continued chafing the wheat. Balarama grew curious and left his play to follow his brother.

Krishna squatted down and watched the snake slithering along the wet drain behind the house. He grew fascinated by the serpent's movements and began to want to imitate it. He crawled into the drain on his belly and began slithering after the snake, imitating it perfectly. Naturally, once Balarama saw Krishna, he wanted to do the same.

When she couldn't spot the boys, Rohini got up and came running over and looked down into the drain to see Krishna and Balarama slithering on their bellies after a snake. For the life of her, she couldn't tell if they were trying to catch the snake or merely imitate it.

Swords and weapons were a special problem. Having seen them being used by men during training, both boys were always eager to imitate their older counterparts. Once, some veterans passing through had left their swords leaning against the side of the house and gone inside to drink some buttermilk. Krishna and Balarama saw the swords lying unattended and took their chance.

The sound of metal clashing drew everyone out of doors. And when they came out, they saw the little boys holding swords twice as tall as themselves, swinging the blades with mad abandon, each blow threatening to lop off one's head or the other's arm or chop off a leg ...

Fire, thorns, birds, jumping from heights ... nothing daunted the boys. They were willing to experiment with anything if left unattended for even a moment. It was as if they felt compelled to explore every possible aspect of mortality first-hand and to experience it for themselves.

They grew up quickly, beginning to play with boys much older than their ages, joining in their games and quickly beating them all. The older boys took this in good spirit, for everyone loved and admired Nanda Maharaja and loved Krishna just as much. But it was Krishna who would soon tire of the predictability of winning each time and desire new challenges.

He would release all the cows from the enclosure at the wrong time, then climb on the fence and sit there giggling as the cows went lowing into the fields, eating more than their share at the wrong time of day, while all the gopas and gopis ran about shouting and blaming one another for leaving the fence open. It took them a while to realize that little Krishna was capable of opening the heavy fence on his own. In fact, Krishna always put Balarama to the task of pushing the heavy fence door open while he shooed the cows out and twisted their tails to make them move faster. So when he was asked if he had played this prank, he would mumble quite innocently and truthfully: 'But I didn't open the fence! It was Bhaiya! He did it!' And of course everyone would turn to Balarama, and Rohini would gather up her son and scold him. What was more, Balarama always took the blame and the resultant scoldings without a whisper of complaint. He would do anything for Krishna.

But the biggest mischief began when Krishna developed a fondness for dahi. He had always loved it and had begun demanding it of Yashoda even when he was of an age when children usually drank only milk. But now that he was old enough to go and take it for himself, he began indulging his taste to absurd limits.

Every night, Yashoda would set a large vessel of dahi to set overnight, meant to feed the entire family the next day. With forty-four people in their family, there would be a very large quantity of dahi.

At one meal, Krishna finished his share of dahi and wanted more. He asked Yashoda who fetched him another serving. Krishna ate this up as well and still wanted more. Yashoda fetched him yet another serving. She kept the servings small so that no food was wasted. But Krishna finished the third helping and still craved more. Yashoda was involved in a very entertaining discussion with her sisters and friends and out of sheer distraction asked Krishna: 'You mean to eat the whole store of dahi from the kitchen?' Having said this, she went back to the discussion.

Now, Krishna was less concerned about the admonition than with the revelation that there was a greater store of dahi kept in the kitchen. Intrigued, he got to his feet and pattered away barefoot through the large house. He seldom went to the kitchen because he rarely needed to go there: Yashoda and Rohini always made sure the boys were fed well and on time.

This part of the house was empty. Everyone was gathered in the living rooms, talking and enjoying the evening hours of leisure after a hard day's work.

Krishna walked alone into the kitchen. He went about looking into various vessels, seeking out the dahi. He searched every last vessel without finding it. Disappointed, he thought that Yashoda-maiya had only said what she did to make him keep quiet whereas the truth was that there was no dahi left.

Upset by this, he started to run back to his mother to tug at her garment and complain to her loudly. Just then, he glimpsed a door ajar and remembered that there was a smaller chamber behind the main kitchen.

He pushed open the door with the fearless boldness of a boy who knows that it is his house and he can do anything he pleases there. He entered a long, narrow chamber which was the pantry and larder area.

There were a few vessels here as well, and he searched them at once. The second one turned out to be a whole vessel filled with freshly set dahi. It was the next day's batch and had set already due to the cool weather. There was more whey on the top than Krishna was used to in his dahi, but it was still dahi!

He dipped his fingers into it, scooping out a little, and tasted it. He had to slurp to keep it from spilling from his mouth. Yummy! He smacked his lips. This was even better than the dahi he had just had after the meal. It was freshly set and he liked the thin layer of cream on top. The dahi Yashoda had just served him had come from the bottom of that day's vessel, so it had been totally devoid of cream.

Krishna thought he would have a few more mouthfuls, then stop. There was such a big vessel of it, Maatr would hardly notice a little missing from one side.

After a few mouthfuls, he still craved more. It was so creamy, so rich, so tasty!

Little Krishna had been scooping out the top layer to get as much cream as possible. This meant that he had to keep going around the side of the vessel. He realized that he had eaten almost a complete circle around the edge of the vessel. It looked like a wheel drawn on the surface of the dahi. Yashoda-maiya would certainly notice the missing dahi in a trice. He had never done anything like that before and had no way of knowing how she might react.

Perhaps if I eat the layer of cream on the inside of the circle, it will all look the same again and Maatr won't notice.

He began scooping the creamy layer from the inside.

Time passed.

A member of the household who passed through the kitchen on his way to the backyard heard the odd sound of Krishna slurping dahi from his fingers but could not figure out what the sound meant or where it was coming from. Turning his head this way, then that, he stood by the kitchen doorway for several moments and finally concluded that it was some rodent digging his way under the house.

'Those rabbits are back again,' he told Nanda as he entered the house. 'I heard one of them trying to burrow through the ground. It sounded like it was gobbling up the mud!'

Nanda thought it odd for rabbits to be digging in that season, but said he would take a look around the next day. Everyone went back to their pastimes.

Krishna finished eating and looked down at the vessel of dahi. He had eaten the full layer of cream from the top now, all the way across. But he had scooped his hand too deep in one or two places, and the level of dahi in those places was noticeably lower than in the rest of the vessel. *Maiya would certainly notice that!*

He decided that if he ate around the whole vessel, taking just enough to level out the surface, it would all look pristine again and Yashoda would not be able to tell the difference.

It will look exactly like it was when freshly set, Krishna told himself, grinning, and set to his task with gusto.

Much later, he sat looking down at the vessel of dahi. Apparently, he had managed to finish the entire thing. All the dahi was gone! He had even wiped the bottom clean with his fingers, then licked every last drop off his fingers.

Now what?

Maiya would surely notice an empty vessel. Perhaps she might think she forgot to set the dahi?

No. Maatr never forgets such things, not ever.

What to do then?

A thought came to him.

Rohini-maiya lived in the cottage next door. Perhaps she had her own store of dahi too? After all, Balarama ate much more than he did and he loved dahi almost as much.

He decided to go check.

Rohini's house was open too, as were all houses in Gokuldham. There were no thieves here because nobody would steal from their fellow Vrishnis. That was true for all of Vrajbhoomi. But there was no vessel of dahi here. Krishna had no way of knowing that Rohini took her dahi from Yashoda's supply, for she was a member of the family too, as was Balarama.

All he could think of was the empty vessel of dahi and what Yashoda-maiya would say once she found it empty.

Krishna decided to try Sawariya-mausi's house next door. The lady in question was at his house, talking with his mother and her friends and sisters right now, so her house was likely to be empty. It was.

And there was a freshly set vessel of dahi in the storage area. What was more, there were other vessels as well. When Krishna checked them out of curiosity, he was surprised to see that they were also filled with freshly set dahi. Seven, eight ... ten full vessels of dahi! He didn't know that Sawariya-mausi sold the dahi she made at the market each day. He childishly assumed that it was all for her and her family. *How much could they possibly eat? One vessel? Two, maybe? Three at most? They don't need so much dahi. I can take one and replace Yashoda-maiya's vessel and Sawariya-mausi won't even notice.*

And even if she did notice, she was hardly likely to blame Krishna for it.

He picked up the vessel. The weight itself was not a problem but the size was an issue. It was a strain for him to pick it up and carry.

Then he thought of something.

What if this dahi doesn't taste as delicious as Yashoda-maiya's? Surely she will wonder why, then.

Besides, he thought, once he took the vessel back home and put it in his mother's pantry, it would be from the same vessel that he would be fed the next day as well. So it mattered greatly to him how the dahi tasted.

He dipped one tiny finger into the corner of the surface just to taste the dahi.

He sucked the finger.

A look of ecstasy came over his face.

'It isn't as delicious, it's better! Yummier!'

He tasted a little more, just to be sure. Then another scoop, to savour the rich, creamy taste again.

Then he saw that he had spoiled one corner of the surface cream, so he decided to eat around the rim to even it out.

Time passed.

Krishna sat in his neighbour's kitchen, eating her dahi.

He lost track of time.

Before he knew it, he was looking down at an empty vessel. Again.

No matter, he told himself. *There's plenty more here.*

Speaking of which ... there was so much there that he could leave several for Sawariya-mausi's family, take one home to replace Yashoda-maiya's dahi and still have a vessel or three to spare.

He decided that there would be no harm in eating a bit more. Just the cream off the top of another vessel.

And so it went.

Some time later, Yashoda realized that Krishna had been gone a long time. She asked Rohini if she had seen him. Rohini frowned. 'He was with you when I last saw him, eating something.' Balarama lay in her lap, fast asleep. Krishna had made him push a boulder uphill several times that day, just to see whether it rolled faster when it was at different points on the hill. He was tired from all that pushing and had fallen asleep immediately after his evening meal.

Yashoda thought back and recalled fetching two or three servings of dahi for Krishna. 'And he wanted more,' she said aloud.

It occurred to her to look in the kitchen, just to be sure.

She looked around but found nobody there.

Then she remembered that she always kept the dahi vessel in the cooler pantry area and looked there.

She saw the empty dahi vessel and knew at once what had happened.

'Look at this,' she said to Rohini and the other ladies who had followed her out of concern. 'He's gone and eaten the whole store of dahi!'

'But where is he?' Rohini asked.

Yashoda thought for a moment, forehead creasing, fist resting on her hip. That rascal Krishna, eating up all the dahi! She would give him a piece of her mind once she found him. 'He must be hiding somewhere,' she said, 'afraid that I will scold him.'

So they began searching the house, looking in all the usual places where Krishna hid. It was a big house and it took a while, even with so many people searching at once, because they were all talking at once and kept going over the same places again and again. Finally they were done and Yashoda was certain that Krishna was nowhere in the house.

'Maybe he's in the cowsheds,' she said. He had hidden there once when he had toppled her brother-in-law's uks cart off the side of a cliff, sending it crashing into the ravine below. 'I just wanted to see if the cart could fly,' he had said by way of explanation when he was finally found.

But he was not in the cowsheds either.

By the time they finished searching there, it was very late at night. There were a lot of cowsheds and a lot of crevices where a little boy could easily hide.

Everyone regrouped, most smelling of cow dung and cow urine, a few – who had been splashed while bending down to search under the cows' bellies – of fresh milk. Krishna had been known to hide in such places.

They began to worry.

By this time, Balarama had woken up due to the commotion.

While everyone was debating where else to look and what else to do, he pushed at his mother's arms, asking to be put down, and when Rohini did, he instantly began walking away in a certain direction.

Rohini caught hold of Yashoda's arm and pointed at Balarama, who was walking purposefully up the road.

Rohini and Yashoda followed him without saying a word. The rest came behind them, also trying to keep silent. When some tried to ask where they were going, the others shushed them loudly. The shushing was louder than the voices.

Finally, Balarama came to a halt in front of a house only two doors away from Yashoda's and Nanda's residence. He looked up at the house as if sensing something. Then he ran in through the open door.

Yashoda and Rohini went in. 'This is Sawariya's house,' said Yashoda.

Looking for Balarama, they went into the house and found him in the pantry off the kitchen.

He was standing and looking down at Krishna.

Krishna, who was sitting in the centre of ten large vessels that had apparently been filled with dahi not long ago.

Nine of which were empty now. Licked clean!

The last vessel was half full and Krishna was working intently on that one now, scooping dahi with both hands and slurping noisily to catch the runny bits. His clothes, hair, face, his entire body was coated in dahi, and he looked like he had fallen into a vessel of dahi or emerged from one freshly set!

He continued eating, not even aware of Yashoda's and Rohini's presence – they were still by the door, peering inside. But he was aware of Balarama's arrival. 'Bhaiya,' he said, pointing down at the dahi. 'Yummy-yummy. Taste, no!'

Balarama sat down at once, and began scooping dahi into his mouth as well.

Yashoda and Rohini looked at each other. They shook their heads slowly, despairingly. Then, unable to help themselves, they burst out laughing together. Great peals of laughter poured from their mouths. Tears of mirth rolled down their faces. The others, still tiptoeing through the house and shushing one another, all heard the laughter and came running.

Krishna heard his mother's laughter and reacted at once.

He jumped to his feet and pointed at Balarama, who stood frozen with his hand inside the vessel of dahi at the sound of the laughter.

'I didn't do anything,' Krishna said loudly and with confidence. 'It was Bhaiya! See! He's eating all the dahi!'

two

The crowd roared in adulation. People even threw money and items of food – anything they had in hand – perhaps not realizing that Kamsa did not fight for money. He fought for glory. And in the past year he had amassed a great deal of it.

The fact showed in the way he was greeted by even the aristocrats, noblemen and kings in Jarasandha's pavilion as he entered. All of Magadha loved him. A record number had turned out to watch the Champion of Mathura play in the day's games, and before it began, one of Kamsa's men had whispered in his ear the figure rumoured to be the total value of the bets placed on that day's game alone. It was a king's ransom.

Kamsa slapped the backs and shoulders of his men as they parted ways. All his teammates had become his dear friends and mates in life as well. Sala, Mustika, Kuta, Tosalaka and Chanura were the closest to him and he treasured the time spent training and practising with them. His participation in this sport had changed his life, just as Yadu had predicted. 'There are only three things in life that drive a man forward,' the old man had said to Kamsa, 'someone to care for who cares about you, something you love to do, and something to aspire towards. Without these three things, nothing is worth anything.'

Kamsa had found someone to care about briefly – Putana – and her loss had unsettled him. But the other two items on that short list had never been his to enjoy. He had never found out what it was he truly loved doing, nor did he aspire towards anything in particular. When young, he had desired to be what his father was, a great and powerful king of Mathura. But once he had achieved that goal and lived the life of a king for a decade or more, it began to seem meaningless and empty. Was this all there was to kingship? What next? And as for a goal to aspire to, he had found nothing else apart from that. That was because all his life he had barely hoped to achieve his first goal, of replacing his father. He had never been able to think beyond that.

But after he had begun playing this sport, he had realized a few important things. One was that the way one reached one's position could be arbitrary and at times dictated simply by one's birth, but no matter how one found it, success changed everyone. It didn't matter that he was the king of Mathura. A king could simply inherit his throne. In a sense, Kamsa had inherited his, after all. But a champion in a sport could only attain that position through talent and effort. Kamsa had excelled at kho to an extent that nobody could have believed possible. But more than simply excelling, he had made the sport itself a national pastime. Nay, an international pastime! For, now they were planning an inter-kingdom tournament with rounds eliminating teams until only the two or three best were left for the final day.

After all, Magadha was no more a kingdom; it was an empire. And an empire needed something to bind its diverse and multiple cultures and peoples together. Jarasandha had seen his soldiers playing the game behind their tents one night several years ago and had arrogated the idea for himself, sponsoring larger and larger games until finally, each time his army camped even for a week, they set up a stadium overnight and held games for all to watch. Jarasandha had intended it to be a means of alleviating the stresses of battle and the inter-tribal rivalries and enmities that often led to late-night gang fights and daggers in the back. But what Kamsa had done was take the same sport and transform it into a national diversion. With himself its national champion.

Now, he had queens fawning on him, princesses eager to offer their virginity to him, lords and merchants betting huge wagers on him and keen to be seen by him and with him for their own reasons. He had the respect and admiration of his own wives, both of whom, he was pleased to note, had bellies heavy with child. But above all, he had the grudging but unmitigated admiration of Jarasandha himself.

The god emperor rose from this throne as Kamsa entered the main pavilion. 'All rise for the champion,' said his father-in-law in his piercing voice. And every last person in the large tent rose and bowed and congratulated Kamsa. Girls ran up and hung flower garlands around his neck until he began to feel like a living garden. Oily looking men with curled moustaches made barely veiled offers to have Kamsa wed their daughters, sisters, aunts, nieces.

When all the hubbub was over, he sat with Jarasandha on the throne dais. Entertainments continued in the hall, but the Magadhan's attention was barely on the nubile dancers or exotic music, said to be from some far western nation named Egyptos.

'You have done well,' Jarasandha said to him. 'I am genuinely impressed.'

Kamsa felt a flush of pleasure. He did not know why he felt such a great satisfaction at hearing Jarasandha praise him, but knew it had something to do with the fact that his own father had never praised him much as a child, and once he had imprisoned the old king, he had taken away any reason to be praised forever. In Sanskrit, there is no separate word for father-in-law. The term is simply father. And he supposed that Jarasandha had come to represent a father-like figure in his life. He had moulded him, prepared him, awakened his rakshasa nature, taken that power from him, transformed him into something else, albeit unwittingly. Jarasandha had been present during all the major turning points in his life, moving him this way, then that, like a piece in a chaupat game. Even this most recent change was Jarasandha's doing. Yadu had somehow known that Jarasandha would present Kamsa with this challenge and would expect him to perform or die, but it was Jarasandha who had put him into the stadium and told him to play. And even now, it was Jarasandha whose opinion mattered to him more than all those screaming crowds and fawning nobles.

'Some day, we should have a bout or two,' Jarasandha added.

Kamsa felt a thrill of elation. Jarasandha prided the sport of wrestling even more than the game of kho. He was reputed to be a master wrestler, perhaps the greatest that ever lived. For him to invite Kamsa to spar with him was a great honour and privilege. It didn't matter if he won or lost; Kamsa would give his front teeth just to be able to lock heads with his father-in-law and show him what he was capable of first-hand.

Perhaps that was just what Jarasandha desired as well.

'There is trouble brewing in Hastinapura,' Jarasandha said, 'and it will affect Mathura sooner or later. I am told that Vasudeva has been in constant touch with Bhishma Pitamah, the old Kuru pitr, sometimes directly, and through his envoy Akrur on other occasions.'

'Envoy? How can Vasudeva have an envoy? He is a rebel in exile!'

'Not to his people. They consider him their king even now. And you the usurper. For that matter, there are factions even within Mathura who consider you a usurper and your father to be the rightful liege of the land.' Jarasandha gestured casually. 'But you know all this already. I am concerned about the events unfolding in Hastinapura and how they will affect us in future.'

Kamsa nodded. He had heard the same things through Pralamba. 'What would you have me do?'

Looking into the distance, Jarasandha was silent for a long moment. When he spoke, his voice was speculative and his tone more sibilant than usual. Over the years, Kamsa had noted that when Jarasandha lapsed into these moods of deep concentration, he often began slurring his words together in this sibilant manner. He wondered if that forked tongue was an indication of a more pervasive serpentine nature.

'It has been a while since we heard from your Slayer, has it not?'

Kamsa nodded grimly. He wanted to hawk and spit but restrained himself. This was not the kho ground. There were rules of etiquette and decorum here. 'The last I heard was of the death of your man Trnavarta.'

Jarasandha continued quietly: 'I think it might be time to step up the pressure again. There are more assassins in Vraj, and they have been biding their time, awaiting my signal. I shall be giving them the go-ahead to fulfil their missions now.'

'You mean ...'

'Slay the Slayer, yes,' Jarasandha said. 'But that is only part of the plan. Regardless of whether they succeed, I want you to do everything you can to harry the Vrishnis.'

'Why?' Kamsa asked because he was curious, not out of concern for the cow herders.

'Because those are Akrur's people. And Vasudeva's. And the longer the rebellion continues, the more complacent they become. It is time to strike the rebels where it will hurt them most: in their homeland. Far from where the leaders are right now.'

Kamsa frowned. 'I thought that was the worst possible thing we could do. That it would only provoke the rebels to renew and intensify their efforts against me. Perhaps even push them into an alliance with my enemies – our enemies.'

'That is why we must do so through other means.'

'Other means …? I don't understand.'

Jarasandha smiled thinly at him. 'Supernatural means.'

Kamsa stared at his father-in-law for a moment, then grinned. He had always had a complicated relationship with his father-in-law. Sometimes he hated this man, sometimes he idolized him. Right now it was the latter.

three

Yashoda churned the milk.

It was among her favourite activities of the day. She found the act of holding the large stirring stick and working it round in a rhythmic, repetitive motion extremely soothing. A household as large as hers, with its constant influx of visitors and extended family dropping by unexpectedly for meals, required a great quantity of yogurt every day. Not to mention those two new mouths that demanded epic servings of yogurt all for themselves. She smiled at the thought of her little Krishna's mischievous antics with the dahi handis and of how, since the day he had sneaked into Sawariya's house and polished off ten vessels full of dahi, he had become notorious in all Gokuldham for being the biggest yogurt eater of the territory. She glanced down into the enormous vat: a goodly part of this would go straight into Krishna's and Balarama's bellies tonight. She could only wonder how much they would consume once they were older. Perhaps they might outgrow their excessive love for dahi by then? Ah, well. She shook her head wistfully, smiling. She could only hope.

She had to use a very large vat and a stirring stick as thick as her own hand and almost as heavy as a boat's oar. This called for all her strength and concentration, and she would have to stand with her feet set firmly apart, her back and shoulders and arms using all their strength to work the stirring stick around in the precise churning action that was needed. Unlike some of the less strenuous chores she performed daily, this one left no room for idle thoughts or distractions. This in itself was soothing, for, to be able to shut out one's many anxieties, worries, concerns, considerations and other mental activities was a great blessing in these troubled times. Then there was the churning itself which called for a certain skill and finesse. If she churned too fast or hard or long, the yogurt would harden too much, and if she did not churn it evenly, it would turn out somewhat lumpy and uneven.

Once she was done with churning the day's milk to yogurt, she dragged the heavy vat into the pantry and turned her attention to her next chore: the churning of the yogurt from the day before into buttermilk. This process was similar to churning milk to yogurt, except that the set yogurt was much harder to churn. She looked forward to the effort. As she began stirring the enormous handi of dahi mixed with water and seasoned with rock salt and some condiments, she grew absorbed in the activity, the world around her fading into oblivion.

Her bracelets tinkled on her forearms, the malati flowers decorating her hair swayed and released their aromatic perfume, sweat trickled down her hairline and temples to be caught by the linen cloth she had wound around her head. Another thicker linen cloth swaddled her broad hips like a girdle. Her earrings swung to and fro each time she completed one turn of the churning. She fell into the hypnotic rhythm she had developed over the years, a song slipping forth from her lips as she worked. It was a lullaby she sang often to Krishna, a favourite one he always wanted her to sing when being put to sleep; but that was not the reason why she sang it now. She sang it because it was the same lullaby her own mother used to sing to her while she churned the buttermilk in her ancestral home. Little Yashoda's nap-time always coincided with the churning, and her mother would nurse her for a while, then set her down beside the churning vat and sing the lullaby to assure her of her presence and love as she worked. Yashoda had fallen asleep so many times to the rhythmic sounds of the churning and her mother's voice singing that song that she associated the two inextricably in her mind. Now, barely aware that she was singing, the song slipped from her lips – and from her heart – as she churned the stirring stick round and round, and a part of her mind fell back, back through the decades into the baby Yashoda lying by her mother's side as she churned buttermilk. And perhaps her mother had heard the same lullaby sung to her as well when she was a baby, and perhaps her mother had churned the buttermilk as she had sung it too. Who could say how many generations of Vrishni women had done the same? As Yashoda sang, generations of her mothers and foremothers sang along with her, each mother to her sleeping child, passing on the gift of tradition and love eternally, down the ages.

Krishna was sleeping inside the house and as Yashoda's song rose, he heard its echoes reaching back through time, linking her to her mother before her, and her mother before her, and so forth to the beginning of their race. He had been sleeping on his back as usual, arms and legs sprawled, but now he flipped over in a quick fluid motion, resting on his elbows and knees, and listened intently to his mother's singing. He could hear not just her voice but the voices of all her ancestors too. He listened to that song of the ages, across time and the barriers of life and death, and felt the maternal love and strength of each of those strong Vrishni women. How could any man ever go to war having ever heard that outpouring of love and nurturing?

Overcome by love, Krishna began crawling towards the rear of the house, then remembered that his body was now capable of independent bipedal movement and pushed himself to his feet. He ran barefoot to where his mother stood churning the buttermilk and grasped her legs from behind. Without pausing in her song or churning, she glanced down and acknowledged him. Briefly. Because her entire attention was focussed on the churning which brooked no distraction. Krishna waited, then went around to her front, tugging at her garment. She sang on, her body swaying as she churned. He looked up at her and felt hunger rise in him powerfully. These mortal bodies, always wanting something or the other. He desired to drink her milk. He could not be denied. The urge was powerful and primordial.

But Yashoda was busy. This was the time she kept for her own self, one tiny bit of the day when she did her chores in solitude, lost in the rapture of her rhythmic churning, or cooking, or the simple pleasure of being able to hear her own mind speak without interference from others around her. The household was enjoying its afternoon siesta and she had cut short her nap in order to give herself this precious time.

Krishna tried hard to get her attention but she was gentle yet firm in her denials. She even picked him up and put him down on the cushion in the corner, urging him to go back to sleep. It was true that he tended to get cranky if he did not get his afternoon nap. Even swayam Bhagwan needed a good nap so long as he was occupying a mere mortal body.

Finally, realizing that he would not leave her alone until he had drunk, Yashoda allowed him to sip from her breast. He drank greedily, wondering at his own thirst, then was lost in the miasma of self-fulfilment that could not be described in words.

Only when floating upon the ocean of payasam, upon the gently sustaining coils of Ananta, his eternal consort Lakshmi beside him, eyes upturned in the transcendental nidra state, had he come close to experiencing this level of fulfilment.

Suddenly, the spell was broken.

Yashoda had placed the day's milk to boil on the fire. She put him down abruptly and rushed to take it off the open flame before it boiled over.

Krishna saw her, saw the boiling milk and understood that she had no choice, she could not continue nursing him and let the milk boil over and burn.

But a part of him could not accept the rejection, the sudden break in his profoundly transcendental state of bliss. Still absorbed in the trivial I-Want self-obsession of his immature human body, he succumbed to that most basic human emotion: disappointment. Angry with Yashoda for denying him the ecstasy of satisfaction, he thrashed about, flying into a rage. Hot tears spilling freely from his eyes, he bit his quivering lips and kicked out blindly. His smallest toe accidentally struck the enormous earthen vat in which Yashoda had been churning the buttermilk. A glancing blow and the vessel shattered to smithereens. Churned yogurt flew everywhere. Yashoda exclaimed in surprise as the pieces and yogurt fell around her, even striking her on the back. She turned from the hot milk to see what had happened.

By the time she looked around, Krishna was gone.

At first she assumed that he had gone back into the house to sulk. At such times, he would grumble to himself, sulk, and suck his thumb until he fell asleep. She cleaned up the kitchen, shaking her head at the waste of all the buttermilk and the vat, but she was in too good a mood to feel upset. Rather, she was amused at her little rascal's tantrums. She decided that today everyone would have to go without buttermilk: they would enjoy hearing the story in place of drinking the delicious drink!

When she was done, she went into the house and changed her apparel. Some of the buttermilk had spilled upon her as well, and she had to wash up and clean herself. By the time she was done, the sound of a commotion outside the house attracted her attention. Passing through the room in which Krishna had been asleep earlier, she realized now for the first time that he was no longer in the house. At once, she put two and two together and surmised that the commotion must surely have something to do with her little tyrant.

Rushing outside, she saw some gopis from the neighbouring houses gathered outside, hands on their hips, chattering and complaining. When they saw her approach, they fell silent at once and looked at one another meaningfully.

'What is it?' Yashoda asked with a mother's perennial concern. 'What has he done this time?'

They sighed and slapped their foreheads and pointed up the road. 'He went in that direction,' said one. 'After he finished emptying out all the dahi handis in this lane.'

Yashoda stared at them. *All* the dahi handis? There were a half dozen houses clustered around her estate. Surely Krishna couldn't have finished all their dahi in such a short while? There was probably some misunderstanding ... *Or some exaggeration that characterizes whatever they insinuate about my little one.*

She ran up the lane in the direction they had pointed. On the way, she met more gopis, as upset as the first ones, coming out of their houses holding the broken pieces of their dahi handis and grumbling loudly about the antics of Yashoda's little rapscallion. They saw Yashoda coming, and one of them hailed her, pointing off the road and into the grove. 'I saw him going that way with his vanarsena,' she said scathingly.

As Yashoda rushed past, another one pointed out that the flowers were coming untangled from her hair. Yashoda ignored her, and ignored her unravelling hair as well as the flowers that were falling out of it. Sweating now in the hot afternoon sun, she ran uphill into the grove that bordered their hamlet. Vanarsena, they had said. What did they mean? Vanarsena referred to the army of simian warriors that Rama Chandra of Ayodhya had raised to invade the island-kingdom of Lanka in order to retrieve his abducted wife Sita in the legendary epic poem Ramayana composed by Sage Valmiki. What did that mean in this context? There were no more vanars left in the world. Like rakshasas and asuras of yore, they had grown extinct in that past age of Treta Yuga, and were no more to be found upon the mortal realm. It was believed that their only purpose had been to serve Rama Chandra, believed by many to be an avatar of Lord Vishnu the Preserver, in his battle against the evil Ravana. Their mission accomplished, they had allowed their species to fade from the earth. How could her baby have found vanars here and now?

The answer came to her in the form of a great chittering as she plunged deeper into the grove. She knew at once what the sound meant. There was a great tribe of monkeys living in this grove and the neighbouring thickets. Monkeys. Not vanars. But easily mistaken for their superior simian brethren who were now extinct. Since Gokuldham, like most of Vrajbhoomi, consisted of rolling hillsides covered with grassy pastures, the monkeys rarely ventured beyond these forested parts. Therefore, their numbers grew dense and considerable at times, and they could become quite fiercely competitive as more of them competed for limited living space.

Right now, judging from the cacophony, it seemed as if all the monkeys in Gokul had gathered in the grove. She could see them in the trees above, their dark shapes thickly clustered on the branches and tree tops, their tails hanging, their mouths open to issue an endless litany of sound. What had upset them so greatly?

She found out the reason soon.

She came into a small clearing where the sun shone through leaves in large fan-shaped beams which caught motes of dust and illuminated the darker recesses indirectly. Within this gloamy illumination sat her little Krishna. Somehow he had managed to drag several large vessels of dahi with him all the way up here. She could not fathom at first how he could have done so. Even Balarama was not in sight this time to share the blame. But she was able to guess the answer from the sight that now met her eyes. Krishna sat on the base of a rice-husking mortar to raise himself as high as possible. Suspended in mid-air around him were several of the dahi handis, most already depleted. Only the last handi contained a little dahi, and even that was disappearing fast. Krishna was scooping out dahi with his own hands and feeding it to his newfound friends.

Vanarsena indeed!

The monkeys had formed a chain of tails and limbs, and were hanging suspended from the largest tree in the grove, dangling down until they could reach their benefactor. The lowest one opened his mouth to receive a scoop of the dahi, which Krishna popped into his mouth, then chittered in thanks and scampered up the tree trunk. He was replaced at once by another eager-mouthed monkey.

Judging from the profusion of empty dahi handis and monkeys gathered, it was obvious this process had been repeated several dozen times already. Yet it was clear that it would hardly be enough to satiate the many remaining monkeys who were still unfed. This was the reason for the cacophony. The monkeys who were farther back in the queue were grumbling loudly about waiting their turn!

Yashoda stood and took in this astonishing sight for a long moment. She could not understand how the dahi handis were suspended in mid-air around Krishna. Then again, if a child of his tender age could pick up and drag so many dahi handis all the way up the hill, it was as impossible for him to make them float in mid-air too! But that was the least of her concerns. What upset her tremendously was not only that he was stealing once again from her neighbours, but that he was doing so not to gratify his own greed but simply to feed monkeys. Monkeys!

This was too much.

She looked around and found a stout stick. She broke off a protruding twig or two from the side, then hefted it. Yes, it would do nicely. She raised it and began making her way towards her little son.

Krishna was totally absorbed in his task. Standing one legged on the mortar, partially lit by the smoky beams of sunlight descending from the high trees, he looked like a performer enacting some epic role in a Sanskrit drama. For an instant, as she approached, Yashoda almost thought she could hear music playing in the background, exactly as there would be if this really were a dramatic performance. Flute music, to be precise. But that was impossible, of course. She had to be imagining it, or perhaps one of the gopas in the valley below was playing the flute to soothe the cows and the wind had carried the sound briefly.

She approached the mortar from behind, waving the stick. Krishna had still not seen his mother brandishing the stick. But the monkeys had!

At the sight of a human waving a big stick, the monkeys lost all interest in the dahi. Shrieking madly and leaping from branch to branch, they began an exodus. Within moments, a majority of them had escaped through the treetops, branches quivering in their wake, leaves drifting free, dust motes swirling in the beams of sunlight around Krishna. Even the monkey who was next in queue for his mouthful suddenly caught sight of Yashoda approaching, mistakenly assumed that her angry gaze and upheld stick were meant for him, and shrieked in panic and scampered away on all fours, leaving a dust trail.

Krishna frowned, puzzled, and peered after him. 'Vanar, come!' he called out plaintively. 'Come eat dahi! Nice-nice tasty-tasty!'

All the vanars had suddenly lost their appetite. Or perhaps they had remembered a monkey marathon they had forgotten about: they seemed to be competing hotly to race one another in a bid to get as far away as possible from the angry mother with the raised stick.

In a matter of seconds, the vanarsena had deserted Rama Chandra, leaving him alone to face his legendary foe.

At last Krishna realized that someone was behind him and turned around. At the sight of Yashoda's angry, perspiring face and the raised stick, he gaped in surprise.

Suddenly, all the floating dahi handis came crashing down to the ground, making a loud racket. Most of them being made of baked earth, they shattered on contact with the ground. Whatever force had been holding them up in the air seemed to have deserted them all of a sudden.

Krishna stared at Yashoda. He gaped at her. He had never seen his mother so angry before. Or brandishing a stick. The stick appeared to be very thick and very strong. If she hit him with it, he had no doubt it would hurt considerably, and he had no wish to feel how hard.

Leaping off the mortar, he jumped down on the ground, and with a yell that rivalled the shrieks of his monkey friends, he ran. The great asura lord gave pursuit, picking up the hem of her garments with her free hand to avoid tripping over it.

The chase did not last long. The boy could have raced ahead at any speed he chose, or flown away, or leapt to another planet if he so pleased, but the fact that he was being pursued by his mother seemed to weigh heavier on him than the fear of her punishment. It was Yashoda's anger that Krishna feared far more than her danda.

And so, not far ahead, he slowed, then stopped. He was crying profusely; his kohl was smeared around his eyes, giving him the appearance of a badger. He stood in the shade of a peepal tree, rubbing his knuckles into his eyes, face wet with tears and slime.

Yashoda came running up, saw him standing there, and stopped to catch her breath. Though she had slimmed down considerably in the past few months, she still had long a way to go before regaining the slender waist she had sported before entering motherhood. As for her hips, they would never return to their pre-maternal narrowness, and excess fat tended to collect there, making it difficult for her to run too fast. She got her breath back and saw how miserable Krishna was: she realized she had scared him badly with the stick. Mischievous though he was, and wilfully though he had stolen the dahi handis and taken them into the grove to feed his monkey friends, no doubt as some kind of retribution for her leaving him when other matters demanded her attention, he was not malevolent or malicious. The instant he saw his mother with a big danda, all the mischief had fled at once. Now, he was genuinely scared.

She stopped for a moment and marvelled at a boy who could face giantesses with poisoned milk and wind demons who could carry you up to the sky, but feared his own mother.

Still, she knew she could not succumb to his tears. She must impress upon her child that he had done wrong. Stealing milk products was the worst crime in Vraj. Everyone made a livelihood from them; they were no less than gold or silver would be to a jewel-trading community, and this time, Krishna had gone too far. He had not even stolen the dahi for himself to eat; he had simply taken it out of petty spite. She could not risk him throwing such tantrums every time he was denied her attention for a moment or two.

So she grasped his arm, seizing him firmly but not roughly, crouched down to his height, and proceeded to explain right and wrong to him. He kept glancing at the stick still clutched in her hand. After a few moments, she threw the stick aside so he would know that she did not mean to strike him. She had never meant to strike him, truth be told.

He listened intently and, as she continued berating him, his tears subsided. By and by, he stopped sniffling and listened to her. In response to her questions whether he would behave himself from now on, he shook his head vigorously. But once the fear was past and he understood that there would be no spanking with that scary big stick, she saw a glimmer of defiance creep back into his dark eyes again. She knew that look well. It meant that he had agreed and accepted her terms ... for now. But he would likely do it again and yet again.

She had to give him some serious deterrent. Something that would rob him of the illicit pleasure of theft and mischief and make him feel it was not worth the punishment.

Her gaze passed over the stick and discarded it. She could never strike him with that thing. Not her baby. Never.

Then she remembered the mortar on which Krishna had been standing when she found him. Walking him back to the scene of crime, she proceeded to tie him to the mortar with a rope. She intended to show him how effectively she could curtail his freedom and restrict his movements. If there was one thing her little Krishna hated, it was being confined to one place for long. This would seem like a far worse punishment than the stick. She passed the rope around his slender little frame, intending to tie him to the mortar.

When she reached the end, she found that the rope was too short to tie properly.

She looked around and saw another length of rope, a pile of discarded hemp rope probably left by someone after some task. She joined the first length to the second and began to tie the rope to the mortar.

Again, the rope seemed too short.

She frowned. This was odd. Adding the new length of rope should have made the whole sufficient to tie. Yet it seemed to have reduced in length rather than increasing! How was that possible?

She tied a third piece of rope – and met with the same result. Once again, the rope was just too short to tie a knot.

Again and again, she continued trying, until finally, she had joined enough ropes together to tie up all the monkeys in Gokuldham. It was to no avail: Yashoda was still unable to tie a simple knot to secure Krishna to the mortar.

She looked at her son.

He was looking into the distance, his chubby cheeks dimpled by a mischievous smile.

She took his chin in her hand and raised his face. She saw the look of mischief on his face. It had not taken long for him to regain his confidence!

'I know you are responsible for the rope not being long enough,' she said softly. 'I saw the way you made the dahi handis float in air, and I know of the things you are capable of. I know what I saw when I looked into your open mouth that day, the day the wind demon attacked you. I know who you really are.'

The look of mischief faded to be replaced by an inscrutable expression. Krishna said nothing, merely listened to his mother's voice.

'I know you can do almost anything you set your mind to,' she said. 'I know that I am merely a mortal woman and no match for your divine abilities …'

He stared at her with great big soulful eyes, as if drinking in her emotions.

'Yet,' she went on after a pause and a sigh, 'I am also your mother in this life. Whatever else you may be in eternity, in this era you are my little son. And I your mother. And in order to be your mother, I must teach you certain things – how to behave, how to respect your elders, how to speak well and live well, how to do well … It is my dharma, just as your dharma in this form is to be a good son. Therefore, my Lord, my divine supreme paramatma, I pray to you, grant me this boon. Let me be your mother. Let me teach you what little I know about being human. Let me show you the way, as I know it. We may or may not enact these roles ever again, but for now, for this one short wink of an eyelash, we are united in this relationship of blood and flesh and nurturing, and I must do my part. Therefore, my Lord, my Bhagwan, I beseech you, work with me. Help me help you. Teach me to teach you. Show me how to show you the way.'

Krishna looked at Yashoda for a long moment, saying nothing. He looked at her tired face, the undone hair, the flowers adorning them wilted and faded and fallen, the dusty garments, and suddenly a look of profound embarrassment and shame came over his little features. He bowed his head slowly, his chin dipping gradually as he came to realize how he had troubled and vexed his mother. It was immaterial if he had intended to do so or not; the fact was he had done so, and that was all that mattered. She was vexed, troubled, harassed and weary. She only wanted to teach him this lesson and then they could resume their loving relationship as before.

He nodded once, acquiescing, then held out his little hands.

Yashoda looked down and saw that the rope had grown in length. Now there was more than enough to tie a knot. She slipped the knot into place, finding the rope seeming to move almost of its own accord and the knot forming perfectly in the first try, without needing any adjustment.

Then she stepped back. Krishna was tied to the mortar now.

But she wondered who had really learnt a lesson: the son or the mother!

four

'I am pleased with you,' Jarasandha said. His voice echoed in the enclosed confines of the stone chamber.

Kamsa felt himself flush with pleasure at the compliment. It took an effort to keep from showing his father-in-law how much he enjoyed being praised by him. It was rare to be complimented by the god emperor, rarer to receive such praise unsolicited. Kamsa wondered what he had done to deserve this particular kudos but held his tongue and waited to hear what Jarasandha said next.

The Magadhan reached the bottom of the stone stairwell and vanished for an instant. Kamsa was close behind him, but by the time he reached the bottom of the stairwell, he found himself unable to see where Jarasandha had gone. He felt a moment of unease: the god emperor was better known for slaughtering people, even his own, rather than complimenting them. Perhaps the kudos had merely been intended to throw Kamsa off his guard. Then he glimpsed a flicker of light from a corner and saw that there was a slanted passageway there. It was virtually impossible to detect unless lit from within, as it was now. Kamsa had to bend over to pass through and even then felt claustrophobic. They were deep within the subterranean chambers of Jarasandha's new city, the resplendent Magadha that Kamsa had seen taking shape a decade ago. They had ridden here half a fortnight ago, and Jarasandha had treated

Kamsa as an equal and a friend all through the trip, introducing him to several of his commanders and kings en route, referring to him with evident pride as his son-in-law. All concerned had treated Kamsa with such deference that he had felt an unexpected surge of satisfaction. Even Ugrasena could not have had so many kings bowing to him during his long reign. That in itself gave him a great sense of satisfaction.

He remembered his father again now as he followed Jarasandha through a long-winding, low-ceilinged passageway to finally emerge into a large stone chamber. Jarasandha dipped the head of the torch into a little channel that ran around the wall of the chamber and the liquid in the channel took flame at once. The fire travelled around the wall and higher still, illuminating the chamber. Kamsa saw that a network of artfully concealed channels had been cut into the stone for the fluid to flow freely. The liquid itself took fire but burned slowly, providing more than sufficient light to see by, yet giving out no smoke or discernible odour. He guessed that was important in an underground chamber with insufficient ventilation where one could easily suffocate with too many lit torches blazing at once.

He marvelled at the architecture of the chamber which was cut entirely from stone. It was artfully designed and executed. Yet he could not fathom the purpose of such a chamber. It was clearly no underground dungeon or place of confinement. What purpose did it serve, then?

Jarasandha smiled at him. 'You are wondering at the function of this place?'

Kamsa nodded.

Jarasandha pointed at the far wall of the chamber. 'Observe.'

The Magadhan began chanting shlokas in the rapid-fire,

self-absorbed tone that Kamsa had heard Brahmins intone so often before. But the language he used was not Sanskrit, nor was he reciting any type of shloka that Kamsa had ever heard before. The very language and form of pronunciation were alien, foreign, unfamiliar to his ears.

He was startled when the far wall of the chamber burst into flames. It was as if the same fluid that ran in the recessed channels had been splashed in great quantities upon the blank stone wall and had caught fire. The very wall seemed to blaze with a brilliant searing green light.

Kamsa covered his eyes from the blinding light. 'What—?' he began.

'That is a vortal,' Jarasandha said. 'The mantras I recited are the key to opening and closing it, but there are other means by which it can be accessed. Some involve the use of devices such as you cannot imagine. But these things do not concern you. All you need be concerned with is that such a thing as a vortal exists and that it can be used at will.'

Kamsa stared at the blazing wall of green flames. 'I don't understand, Father,' he said. He had taken to calling Jarasandha father these past few days – at Jarasandha's own request. It seemed to roll naturally off his tongue. 'What is this thing, this … vortal?'

Jarasandha explained it to him.

Kamsa goggled.

'A portal for travelling from our world to other similar worlds?'

'Yes,' Jarasandha said, 'worlds that are variations of our own. Infinite worlds, infinite variations.'

Kamsa shook his head. 'Forgive me, Father. I do not understand.'

Jarasandha chuckled softly. 'I should have expected that. Yes, I do understand and it does not matter one whit. The beauty of the vortals is that you do not need to understand them in order to use them. You only need know how to use them, and that is something I can show you easily enough.'

He stepped towards the wall of green fire. Flames flickered and rolled and crackled upon the stone wall, emitting the most peculiar mossy green luminescence Kamsa had ever seen. 'Come,' Jarasandha said, 'let us pass through. What I have to show you can only be understood after you enter the vortal.'

Kamsa swallowed. He could face warriors twice his size, take on armies, battle enemies by the dozen. But this ... this was ... 'Sorcery,' he blurted, unintentionally speaking the word aloud.

'Perhaps,' Jarasandha said calmly, 'for what else is sorcery but a highly advanced form of science, an art whose rules we are yet to learn. But even if it is sorcery, it is of a form that can be used to our advantage.'

'Must I ...' Kamsa ventured to ask, then paused, swallowing thickly. 'Must I pass through it?'

'Yes,' Jarasandha said casually. 'Because if you do not, I shall tear you limb from limb right here and now, and eat your vitals. Have I made myself clear enough?'

Kamsa forgot his terror of the strange green wall of fire and turned his attention to his father-in-law. He saw that Jarasandha meant every word he had uttered: he would literally tear Kamsa to pieces and eat his organs, probably while Kamsa was still alive enough to feel the excruciating agony. Kamsa's newfound body density made it impossible for almost any other human being, including the formidable Crooked Jaw, to so much as squeeze his tendons, let alone break his bones or cause real harm, and it was possible that if he fought Jarasandha one on one, he might win … but then again, he might not. And he was not sure he wanted to risk it.

Suddenly, he didn't feel too afraid of the green wall of fire. Whatever it looked like, it probably wouldn't burn him. After all, Jarasandha meant to go through it as well, and he would hardly condone burning his own skin or flesh. Besides, Kamsa had no reason to think his father-in-law meant him bodily harm – not unless he refused to obey his orders.

'I shall do as you say, sire,' he replied and stepped towards the vortal.

'Follow me,' Jarasandha said quietly as he reached out and touched the green wall of flame with one hand. Kamsa watched in amazement as Jarasandha's hand passed through the flames and disappeared from view. 'And we shall ensure the destruction of the Slayer and his entire clan very shortly.'

Then Jarasandha stepped through the wall of green fire and passed from sight.

Without giving himself time to think or question what he was doing, Kamsa followed him.

five

Kamsa cried out in alarm.

He was surrounded by dense rock. From the look of it, the rock and soil here had not been disturbed in millennia and lay exactly as it had formed through aeons of accumulation. In the moments that followed, Kamsa could gather only one thing ...

We are buried! he cried.

Jarasandha turned back to look at him and laughed. *Do not fret. You will come to no harm here. In fact, you are not truly here at all, merely a wraith, a wisp of yourself. We are both no more than ghosts in this realm, for this is the plane of Narada.*

Kamsa forgot his shock and bewilderment and looked up. *Narada? Narada-muni?*

Yes. Look at me, Jarasandha said. He held up his hand. Kamsa saw that Jarasandha's entire body had acquired a rim of fiery greenish flame, as if it had caught fire from the wall of green fire through which they had passed. Jarasandha's upheld hand sizzled with the same eerie flame, flickering even in the webbing between his fingers. *Now look at yourself.*

Kamsa looked. His body too was ringed with the same greenish luminescence.

Jarasandha waved a hand at the nearest rock. His hand passed right through it without any effort, and seemed quite unharmed. *You see?* he continued, demonstrating by punching harder, then moving his entire body forward to show how easily he could pass through the solid bedrock of this subterranean plane. *Like ghosts!*

Kamsa followed him hurriedly, not wishing to lose sight of his father-in-law. He wondered what would happen if he were stranded in that plane alone. He had no wish to learn the answer.

Jarasandha moved freely through the underground, travelling in a slightly upward gradient now. Kamsa did the same, his stomach still feeling queasy as he passed through entire layers of earth and stone and even underground water. He thought he felt colder in the place he was, and when he passed through the pooled underground water, he was certain he felt a faint sensation of … wetness? Damp? But Jarasandha was right. He could not actually feel things as usual. It was more his mind telling his body that it ought to be feeling such things.

Our actual physical bodies lie back there in the underground chamber. That is why I keep the vortal chamber out of view – so that my body can be safe when I travel to other realms. You have already seen how securely I locked the numerous doors and gates to the subterranean chamber. No harm will come to our physical selves while we travel. And no harm can come to us here. Because, you see, my son, we are not actually here. Only our consciousness extends into this realm of Narada. We are probing this place only with our minds.

Kamsa understood the words Jarasandha was speaking, but not their entire purport. He made out that they were safe, they were locked in, they were travelling, and they were not actually in the place they were inhabiting; they were only occupying it mentally. He agreed whole-heartedly – anyone who attempted such things would have to be mental!

Jarasandha continued explaining things as they went forward. He was still talking when he suddenly vanished. Kamsa had another moment of heart-stopping shock when he thought his father-in-law had abandoned him in the hellish realm forever. All manner of thoughts passed through his mind, mostly related to karma and wicked deeds and the likelihood of hell for one such as himself. Then he emerged from the stone-bounded darkness of the underworld into the open air beneath the open sky and clouds and the sun, and saw Jarasandha only a short distance away. His heart flooded with relief.

You must see this, Jarasandha said. *But be very quiet and as still as possible. So long as we do not agitate the ether, we are invisible; but if we move or speak or feel violent emotions, he will sense us. That would not be good. In this plane of existence, he is as a god. After all, this is his realm, created by him for his purposes.*

Who was he talking about? Kamsa wondered. Then he looked over Jarasandha's shoulder and saw for himself.

Narada-muni! In the flesh!

Kamsa started forward, anger rising. *You lied to me! You—*

A hand stronger than a hundred elephants caught hold of his neck in a vice-like grip. Not only his voice, his breath too was choked off abruptly. He felt his windpipe being crushed. So powerful was Jarasandha's grip, he had only to squeeze a little harder and Kamsa's neck would snap. Kamsa was shocked out of his wits. It had been a while since anyone had been able to lay hands on him in this fashion. His unique ability had made him believe himself to be invulnerable. But clearly Jarasandha was far, far more powerful than he was. The single-handed grip the Magadhan exerted on Kamsa's throat was more powerful than anything Kamsa had experienced before. Kamsa's eyes bulged as the life ebbed from his body. He felt his vision blurring, then turning dark. He realized for the first time in over a decade that he was not beyond the reach of mortality, after all. It was a revelation.

His father-in-law's face was bestial, animalistic in its intensity. His nictitating eyelids flashed sideways to reveal serpentine eyes that flickered shut and open repeatedly. The forked tongue flickered between those thin lips, and the skin itself appeared mottled and cracked and veined like snakeskin that had aged a millennium or two. *I. Said. Be. Quiet. Be. Still.*

Suddenly, he felt himself being released. By degrees, his vision returned, and so did his breath, and with them came life. Kamsa fell forward, gasping and choking, but suddenly very conscious of his own actions and careful not to make any noise. He recovered quickly. His body healed instantly, if it had been harmed at all.

He looked up at Jarasandha, who glanced down at him scornfully. *I am sorry, Father. I did not mean …*

Jarasandha gestured dismissively. *No apologies. You cannot suffer harm in this place, nor die as you might have assumed. But you can feel and suffer. Remember that the next time you disobey me.*

Kamsa got to his feet. *I saw the Brahmin and lost my head.*

Jarasandha nodded. *I have the same reaction when I see a Brahmin, any Brahmin. But you must learn to control it. We shall kill many Brahmins in time, you and I. That is one of the reasons we were given this rebirth. But there are other tasks equally important. This trip is to ensure that that larger mission is fulfilled successfully. Do you understand?*

Kamsa nodded.

Jarasandha looked at him for a long moment. The Magadhan's face and appearance had turned normal as before, and his snake-like inner nature was concealed beneath the mortal garb once more. But it lurked thinly beneath the surface, ready to lunge out at any instant. Kamsa berated himself for forgetting that, even for a moment.

Very well, then, Jarasandha continued. *Let us continue. Our task here is simply to observe, nothing more. We must not attract the attention of the one who created this plane, or he will unleash more grief upon us both than even I could unleash upon you. Do you follow, Kamsa?*

Kamsa nodded vigorously.

In this plane, he is supreme. For it is not a real realm or plane of existence in the usual sense. It is merely a vortal between worlds. And Narada is a master of vortals. As a messenger to the devas, he needs to pass quickly from one plane to another, one time to another, one part of space to the other, and this is the quickest way. He has created this plane from the amalgam of the effluents of all his trips, and uses it to observe various events and to plan his next move. The reason why you were about to lunge at him was because you felt he had betrayed you, am I right? You felt he had forewarned you about the Slayer's impending birth so that you could prevent him from being born or kill him at birth itself, and when you realized that the Slayer had survived after all and is still alive and growing up safely somewhere, and will some day come to challenge and attempt to kill you, you felt that Narada had lied to you. Isn't that so?

Kamsa stared at his father-in-law in amazement. *Exactly! But how—?*

I have known since the beginning, Kamsa, Jarasandha said quietly. *But had I told you of events that were to happen in the years ahead, you would have either dismissed my warnings or suspected my motives…* He shot Kamsa a shrewd glance. *… As you do even now. For that is how a conqueror thinks – suspect everyone, trust no one. But do not fret. I would expect nothing less from you. After all, I taught you that outlook. Trust no one, not even me. In life, as in death, you are alone. Such a thought process is the only way to triumph over the world. But as for Narada …* Jarasandha glanced in the other direction. *… He is only one player in a much larger game of gods and kings. He told you of the prophecy not to help you but to serve his own ends. It was your folly that you assumed he was acting in your interests and advising you. In fact, he intended the exact opposite. He was steering you towards your destruction!*

Kamsa stared. *But … he told me about the Slayer!*

Yes, and what good did it do you? Did he tell you where and when and how the eighth child would be born? Did he tell you how he could be killed? Narada does know these things, yet he never shared such information with you.

Kamsa's mind boggled with the implications. *But he told me to seek you out! We would never have met if it were not for him.*

Jarasandha chuckled and shook his head. *My envoy was already on the way to Mathura to request you to come to Magadha. My alliance with you was a foregone conclusion. All Narada did was insert himself into your life at an opportune time in order to give you the illusion that he was helping you.*

Kamsa frowned, then grew angry again. His fists clenched and he raised them to pound the earth before remembering that it would be futile in this plane. He let his hands fall to his sides again, and they fell uselessly through the grass on which he sat.

Jarasandha held out a hand. Kamsa took it and rose to his feet. Jarasandha put his hand on Kamsa's shoulder. *That is why I brought you here today. It was time you learnt of Narada's duplicity. And of the larger game being played in which the Brahmin, you, I, and even the mythical Slayer himself are but participants.*

He began walking again, his arm still around Kamsa. *Come. Let me show you.*

Krishna's antics became the talk of Gokuldham. No matter how destructive the pranks played by the little dark one and his milk-fair brother, people always forgave them. After the incident with the stick, Yashoda took to disciplining Krishna each time he misbehaved. She would never raise a hand on him or use too intense a tone and loud a voice, because she sensed that these were things Krishna did deliberately and knowingly. Some part of him knew they were things he was not supposed to do, and that was all the more reason for him to do them. They were his way of getting her attention or the attention of the other gopas and gopis. He thrived on attention. At times, when caught in some act of mischief, or when a crowd gathered to berate his latest activity, he would start dancing. And soon enough, the angry voices would fade and be replaced by amused exclamations as everyone marvelled at his agility and sense of rhythm. His dark feet would pound the dust, his body spinning and twirling at impossible angles, as he would dance with a pace and perfection none other could match. Even the most accomplished dancers of Gokul gaped in amazement and admiration. Krishna's dance was a thing to behold.

And always, accompanying the dance would be the sound of flute music. The same haunting melody that Yashoda had heard the first time in the thicket. And just like on that occasion, no one would be able to make out where the music was coming from or who was playing it. And since the flute was the patent musical instrument of the Vrishnis, used to herd cows, soothe sick ones, and even to coax dry ones into yielding milk, nobody gave it much thought. But Yashoda began to realize that the flute music was coming from Krishna himself. Somehow, miraculously, impossibly, he was playing the flute and dancing at the same time – even though no flute was ever visible! How this could possibly be, she did not know. But like so many other things involving Krishna, she learnt not to question it and to simply accept. The music itself was so beautiful, so mesmerizing, that nobody cared much about its origin or source; men and women simply stopped whatever they were doing and listened, watching as the little dark child's bare feet trampled the dust and his body spun round and round until it seemed as if the very earth spun with him – or because of him. As if it were due to his dance that the planet itself spun on its axis, and because of the angle at which he leaned while dancing that prithvi itself tilted at that peculiar angle while spinning. He seemed to be the Coriolis effect personified, the one who made worlds spin and Creation exist.

This was the beauty and magic of Govinda's dance.

On one occasion, he wanted fruit. He loved to eat fruit, though not as much as he loved buttermilk and curds – nothing compared to those divine foods. And there was no fruit in the house. So he picked up a fistful of grain and went to the fruit-seller in the market, meaning to exchange the grain for the fruit. This too his mother had taught him after the incidents with the dahi handis. 'People depend on selling or trading these items to earn their keep and feed themselves,' she explained to him patiently. 'By taking them without paying for them, we are depriving those people of their means of living. We must always pay a price for everything we consume.'

Krishna did not know how much the fruit would cost and it did not occur to him that even a fistful of grain – especially a tiny fistful like his – would hardly compensate for the fruit he desired. But he remembered to take the fistful, at least. But by the time he reached the fruit-seller, the grain had run out through his fingers and barely a few grains remained on his sweaty palm. He held it out and knew that it would be much too little to pay for the fruit. Even with his little brain – for, as a mortal, he was a babe and subject to the limitations of his body and age – he realized that such tiny grains could hardly compensate for such big fruits. The last time he had seen his mother buy fruit, she had handed a sack of grain that was about the same size as the basket of fruits she had received in exchange. Now he had almost no grain to offer and he was determined to prove to Yashoda that he did not mean to steal or deprive other people of their means of living. What else could he offer that would compensate for the fruits he wished to buy? Finally, an idea came to him and he smiled to himself.

Yes, that would do nicely!

The fruit-seller was busy bargaining with another customer and did not notice little Krishna at once. There was some question about whether or not the fruits were fresh. When she finished and the other customer moved on, carrying a small basket of her purchases, little Krishna piped up from below her line of vision.

'Maatey,' he said, for he had been taught to address all women as 'mother' unless told otherwise, 'how many fruits will this buy me?'

The fruit-seller looked down at the little boy's closed fists. He opened them and showed her the contents.

'Deva!' she exclaimed, attracting the attention of the whole market. 'Where did you get those?'

Attracted by the commotion, other customers and even vendors came to see what was going on. The instant someone spotted little Krishna, word spread, and within moments a crowd had gathered to witness what new mischief Nanda Maharaja's and Yashoda-devi's son was up to now.

'What is it, Malani-devi?' asked one of the bystanders.

'Look,' said the fruit-seller excitedly, pointing to Krishna. 'Look at what he is offering to pay me for my fruit!'

Everyone looked. And was flabbergasted. For in his two little fists, Krishna had a small fortune in precious stones. Sparkling diamonds, scintillating rubies, pearls, emeralds … It was a scattering of the choicest gems any of them had seen.

'Where did you get these?' someone asked Krishna.

By this time, Krishna knew that something had gone amiss. He could only think that they were all so agitated because they thought he had stolen the gems, which he had not, of course. He had simply used the power of his mind to turn the remaining grains in his fist into the kind of gems he knew his mother liked. But he also knew he could not say that to these people because mortals did not believe anyone could do such things. So he tried to be as truthful as possible: 'I got them from the sack in my mother's kitchen,' he said. 'I didn't steal them!'

Everyone goggled at the thought. They knew Nanda Maharaja was well off. But surely not *that* well off! 'How many do you have in the sack in your mother's kitchen?' they asked.

'Oh, lots!' Krishna said, mistakenly thinking that if they thought there were plenty more where these came from, they would see that a handful did not matter much. 'There are many sacks ... Hundreds of sacks! Thousands!'

Everyone laughed. Now they knew he could not be telling the truth. Even King Kamsa the Usurper in Mathura did not possess thousands of sacks of precious gems. Once again, it was assumed that Krishna had been up to his usual mischief and had filched the gems from somewhere.

One wag cried out a closing comment that had everyone in splits: 'Malani-devi,' he said to the fruit-seller, 'you should have kept quiet and taken the payment! Nobody would ever dare to have bargained with you about your fruits! You could always say that you had once sold a basket to Krishna for a king's ransom in precious stones!'

Even Krishna laughed with the crowd, though he did not quite understand why everyone was laughing.

From time to time when he was naughtier than usual – which usually meant that he had caused others to become overly upset or irate at his antics, instead of causing them to laugh as they had over the gems and fruits – Yashoda would gently lead him to the place where the mortar was kept, and tie him to it as she had done that day in the grove. The tying did not harm or cause him any great inconvenience and she never left him tied too long. It only served the purpose of restricting his freedom and reminding him that he needed to correct his behaviour. Krishna understood this and complied without protest, even when he did not understand what he had done wrong. Yashoda always explained his fault to him, patiently, and answered any questions he had, but even so, he often had difficulty differentiating between the things mortals considered incorrect, inappropriate or wrong, and the things they accepted as part of natural behaviour. After that first day in the grove,

Yashoda understood that it was only Krishna's compliance that enabled her to tie him up and for his movements to be restricted by the mortar, but it was the lesson that mattered, not the danda. If she could teach him without waving the stick, she would do so, even if it meant teaching him ten times to understand what he might learn in a single beating with the stick. For the lesson which was learnt through infliction of pain, suffering or coercion was no different from the learning acquired by a slave or a dog. It was only when one learnt willingly that true knowledge could be acquired.

But then an incident occurred which made Yashoda realize that even this mild punishment was no longer useful. It was also the incident that changed the lives of all who lived in Gokuldham and Vrajbhoomi forever and led to the great exodus of the Vrishnis.

seven

The mortar had been moved that day, and been placed in a different part of the backyard of Yashoda's house. There were two arjuna trees beside it, growing close to each other and leaving just enough space for a child to slip through, but not enough for a grown person to pass. Krishna was in one of his stubbornly mischievous moods that day, not just doing mischief but acting defiant about it. In times to come, even Yashoda would have no recollection of what his fault had been on that occasion, because the events that followed were more memorable. The only bit she remembered was that she had punished her son as usual and that it was Krishna's attempt to drag the mortar that made her decide she needed to escalate the penalty. Because of this, Yashoda decided to tie Krishna to the mortar in such a way that he was on one side of the arjuna trees and the mortar on the other. The mortar blocked one way, and if he tried to drag it the other way, the trees would impede his efforts.

'Now wait here and think about the mischief you did until I finish my chores,' she scolded him before leaving.

Krishna sat sullenly for a while, arms folded across his chest, eyes crossed in a sulky expression, lips pouting. Feeling drowsy as he often did when overcome by emotion, he fell asleep without meaning to, and in a while was leaning against one of the arjuna trees, eyes closed and thumb in his mouth, soothing himself to an unconscious state.

Half asleep, he opened his eyes and found himself in a different place and time.

He was on the side of a great mountain, in a grove of extraordinary beauty. The colours of the flowers and fruits and leaves, the quality of the air he breathed, the crystal clarity of the water in the waterfall and river nearby, all testified to it being some supernormal plane. The beauty of the vista he viewed was overwhelming.

You are on the slope of Kailasa, said a voice. Krishna turned to see an ancient man with long, flowing white beard and red ochre garb. *This is the sacred grove called Mandakini. We are in the shadow of your friend and fellow immortal, Mahadev.*

The old Brahmin indicated the top of the mountain. Krishna looked up and saw a snow-crested peak that seemed as familiar as the backyard of Yashoda's and Nanda's house. *He is engaged elsewhere, as are Maatey Parvati and their sons Kartikeya and Ganesha, which is why it was I who came to see what the commotion was about.*

The instant the old Brahmin uttered the word 'commotion', Krishna heard sounds of laughter and splashing. He turned to look down at the river below, at a still pool formed by the overflow from the cascade. There were several people there, splashing about merrily and making a great deal of noise. Even from where he stood, Krishna could see that they were naked as the day they were born.

They are Nalakuvara and Manigriva, sons of Kubera, treasurer of the devas, Narada said. Krishna knew the old Brahmin's name was Narada although he did not know how he knew it. It was as if all knowledge was coming flooding back into his mind just as readily as the glacial river water was cascading down that waterfall below. *They have consumed too much varuni and thought it would be good sport to come and frolic with the gandharvas and apsaras who dwell here.*

Krishna glanced down again and made out two male forms among the score or more of female bodies cavorting in the still pool below. They all appeared to be enjoying themselves greatly.

Their enjoyment of pleasures is not in itself a sin. What is so detestable is the impunity with which they do so with women other than their own wives, in a place reserved as a sacred sanctuary, without the permission of the owner, in a state of such intoxication that they can barely stay conscious. And most offensive of all is the fact that they act thus only because they are empowered by the considerable wealth of their father. There is no quality of rajas that I find more offensive than pride of wealth. The earning and accumulation of riches is a matter of karma and is irrelevant in the larger scheme of things. But when people pride their riches over all else, even common sense and decency, they lose their humanity. To see these two young men act thus indecently and think they can get away with it because they are the spoilt sons of a rich father is unacceptable to me. Therefore I shall curse them. It shall be their fate to remain naked as they are now, and to stay in a state of immobility for a hundred years, until they are freed from my curse by none other than you, son of Vasudeva. And that time has now come.

Almost at once, the landscape before Krishna's eyes changed. Gone was the idyllic beauty of Mount Kailasa, abode of the Three-Eyed One, and in its place was Yashoda's backyard again: with the two arjuna trees in front of him. Krishna looked around and saw that Narada had vanished as well.

He sat up and looked at the trees. They were stout and old, and looked like any arjuna tree he had seen. But he knew now what they truly were.

'It is your lucky day,' he said to the trees, patting each one gently with his baby hands as he stood up. 'Your time of danda has ended and I am to free you now.' And he began to pull with all his might. The mortar moved forward several inches until its edges struck the two trees. There it held fast. Krishna knew that the force required to pull it free was more than what a single horse could exert. Perhaps two or four horses might do it, pulling together and using strong ropes. But he had no horses at hand, and Narada-muni's words had been quite clear. It was up to him, son of Vasudeva, to free these two punished souls.

eight

Jarasandha and Kamsa watched as Narada stood enjoying the sight of little Krishna tugging at the mortar. As Krishna strained his little mortal body, the ropes binding him to the mortar began to slowly stretch and then fray. He saw this and stopped pulling for a moment. Then, taking firm hold of the mortar itself, he began to pull at it with all his might, trying to push it through the gap between the two arjuna trees. There was no room for the mortar to pass, of course. Yet the force Krishna exerted was so great that the mortar began to pull at the trees themselves.

A great cracking noise arose, and with a huge heave, the arjuna trees began to emerge from the ground, their roots unseated by Krishna's force. With a powerful tug, he leveraged the mortar to pull both trees out by their roots. It was an astonishing sight, since even the mortar was twice as high as the little dark-skinned boy. As for the trees, they towered over him, ridiculously tall and strong.

Kamsa could not imagine what strength it must take to uproot the trees. He had smashed many trees since he had acquired his new abilities, but to uproot them in this fashion? Both trees emerged from the ground, their roots, clotted with clods of earth, trailing for several yards. Dust rose up in the air and both the trees came crashing down to the ground on either side of Krishna, sending up a great noise of timber cracking.

Kamsa flinched as he saw people approaching at a run. Jarasandha smiled at his nervousness and patted his shoulder. *They cannot see us. We are watching through Narada's vortal, and Narada himself cannot be seen by anyone on earth at this time. And so long as we remain still and do not evoke too much emotional disturbance, even Narada will not sense our presence here. We are merely ghost observers.*

Kamsa nodded, reassured but still unnerved by the fact that there were people in front of him whom he could clearly see and hear but who could not sense him in turn.

Yashoda came running up, thinking the worst had happened. She was relieved beyond words to see Krishna standing safely, the remnants of the ropes dangling from his arms and waist. The dust cloud behind him had partially settled to reveal the two fallen trees with their roots exposed, and the mortar which had been crushed under the trees when they fell. It was incredible to conceive that her little son could have brought down those two great trees; yet from the first instant she had no doubt that this was indeed the case.

'Krishna!' she cried, embracing him. He was coated from head to foot in dust, turning his jet-black skin powdery white in colour. 'What have you done this time?'

He smiled at her. 'Maatr, I freed the sons of Kubera!'

She looked in the direction he was pointing, at the two fallen trees. People had gathered around, talking agitatedly, but Krishna was pointing where nobody was looking, at the ends of the roots of the two trees. Yashoda saw a shimmering miasma gathering, as if some preternatural sap were oozing from the tips of the roots and collecting into two separate masses. As she watched, the masses coalesced to form two ghostly humanoid shapes. She was even able to discern that they were men, two young men clad in rich robes and jewels. These two ghostly shapes, barely as substantial as the dust settling around them, joined their palms together and bowed before Krishna.

Supreme yogi, she heard them say, and knew at once that they were speaking not in sounds but in words only her mind could hear, just as Krishna had spoken to her when he was younger. They continued: You are the Paramatma. All of Creation is merely your body. You are the ultimate controller of the senses, souls, essences, and corporeal forms of all entities. You are Kala itself, time infinite. You are swayam Bhagwan. You are none other than Vishnu, the indestructible Preserver. You are the mahout and the prakriti. You contain rajas, sattva and tamas within your being. You are the overseer of all things, the supremely knowledgeable One, the uncapturable, the personification of almighty Brahman itself. In this your amsa, you have blessed us wrongdoers by freeing us of our earthly prisons, leaving us free to return to our true forms and resume our celestial duties. Pray, give us permission to depart now, Lord. We are eternally grateful to you and remain your servants. We pray for the forgiveness of your servant Narada as well, and deeply regret the offence we caused him and Mahadeva as well by violating the sanctity of the sacred grove.

And as Yashoda looked on in wonderment, her little Krishna cried out, 'Go now! You are forgiven.'

And after circumambulating her son with folded palms, the two guhyakas vanished without a trace.

Only then did Yashoda become aware of the great commotion around her.

'Another asura attack!'

'Once again Nanda's and Yashoda's little one was spared only by the grace of Vishnu.'

'Look how close he came to being crushed by the falling trees.'

'Look at the state of the mortar!'

The voices rose in a cacophony, blocking out Yashoda's protests and attempts to explain. She tried repeatedly to explain that it was only Krishna who had pulled down the trees but, of course, nobody would believe her.

Finally, Krishna himself put a hand on her head and said affectionately, 'Maatr, do not trouble yourself. They will believe what they believe to be true. But you know the ultimate truth.'

She was appeased by his words and his childish wisdom, but still felt troubled. 'Yes, my son, but they are very upset. There is talk of migrating out of Gokuldham ... even leaving Vrajbhoomi and going into exile. They fear that this is yet another sign that we Vrishnis are no longer welcome in this land. They mean for us to make an exodus! Your father Nanda's friend Upananda has been advocating it from the very first incident of the cart breaking, and now, given the current mindset of our people, he might even prevail. This may well be the incident that provokes our clan to leave our beautiful homeland and go into exile!'

Krishna nodded, understanding all, and patted his mother lovingly. 'So be it,' he said. 'Let what will be, be.'

She stared at him.

He grinned mischievously. 'How do you know it is not what I intended from the very beginning?'

She was thunderstruck. Could it be possible? That Krishna wanted them to leave Vraj and Gokul? 'You mean ...' she began.

He shushed her with a raised finger. 'Let us not speak further, Maatr. Who knows who might be listening? Come, take me home now and bathe me. I wish to be clean and fresh before I drink of your milk again. And I am thirsty enough to drink all your milk today!'

And he took her larger hand in his own, clasping it tightly, and turned her homewards.

nine

Jarasandha cursed as their view of Krishna and Yashoda faded, and even Narada turned away, looking smug and satisfied.

What is it? Kamsa asked. He was still reeling from the sight of the Slayer. That child? That little tyke? He was the prophesied one who would some day kill him, Kamsa? He could barely believe it. Yet he had witnessed the felling of the trees with his own eyes – or whatever passed for his eyes in this incorporeal plane – and he knew that what he had seen was no little boy.

He knows something, Jarasandha said. *He is looking forward to going away with his clan! That is not the way it was supposed to be.*

Kamsa frowned. *How was it supposed to be?*

The attacks by the assassin squad I gave you were meant to chase the Vrishnis out of Vraj with their tails between their legs, frightened and scared, seeking sanctuary.

Kamsa thought for a moment. *Is that not what is about to happen? They are going into exile now, are they not?*

Yes, but that little God of the mortals, he is up to something! He knew all along that they would go into exile and he is not afraid of it. He looks forward to it, even takes credit for it!

But what does that mean? Kamsa asked.

It means that our traps and snares set in the place of exile might be foreseen by him, Jarasandha snarled. As he spoke, he dove into the ground. Kamsa followed. They were travelling back to the subterranean spot from where they had entered the realm, he knew now. Back through the gateway that Jarasandha called a vortal, to their own world. Kamsa would be relieved to return there; he did not care overmuch for supernatural tourism.

I see, he said, understanding suddenly and filling with bright, shining hope. *You intended this all along. You gave me Putana and the other assassins to send after the Slayer, knowing that they would fail but would serve a greater purpose: to shepherd the Vrishnis into a trap?*

Jarasandha shrugged as they passed through giant boulders and stratified fossils. *I did not know for certain they would fail. I hoped they might succeed. But if they did not, yes, there was a larger plan in place. And yes, that larger plan was to shepherd the human herd into a place where we could devour them as calves in a den of wolves.*

And that is precisely what is happening now, Kamsa observed. *Yet Krishna said he did not fear it, he even seemed to welcome it.* It was strange saying the name of the Slayer, but even as he said it, he knew that it was right. This was indeed born of his sister's body, the one who was prophesied to kill him. He could feel the blood they shared the instant he spoke the name, feel the connection that bonded them eternally. *Therefore, it would seem that he is not aware of the traps you have laid in that new place of exile.*

Jarasandha slowed down; Kamsa did likewise. Jarasandha was silent for a moment, then looked sharply at Kamsa. *You are right. Perhaps he welcomes it because he mistakenly believes the attacks will continue in Gokul. Perhaps he does not know of the dangers awaiting him in exile! Not only him, but his people as well, for as you have seen, the key to destroying a leader or saviour is to destroy those who regard him as one. Destroy faith and you kill a god. For what is a god without anyone to believe in him?*

He clapped a hand on Kamsa, hitting him hard enough to knock out his breath momentarily. *You may be right. Perhaps the Slayer is naive enough to fail to see my larger plan. He foolishly thinks that this is the best way for his adopted human family to survive!*

Kamsa grinned. It was rarely that he made his father-in-law happy, yet he appeared to have done so for the second time today. That was an achievement. *And now you will tell me all about your plans to ambush him and his people in the place of exile, and how your strategy will finally end the life of the Slayer and rid me of his menace, yes, Father?*

Jarasandha nodded indulgently. *I shall, Son.*

And they passed through the vortal, back to their world.

ten

Yashoda could still not accept that her entire clan should be forced into exile. She loved Vraj and Gokul dearly, and the thought of leaving broke her heart. But she was reassured by Krishna's words as well as by Nanda's assurances that this was the inevitable course of action.

'Even in council,' Nanda said gently, 'all the elders agree that these attempts on our son's life are signs that must be heeded. We must make this move. But have no worry, my beloved. The place we go to is no less beautiful and resplendent than our beloved Gokuldham.'

'Where are we going?' she asked, curious.

'A place called Vrindavan,' he replied.

'The legendary garden grove?' she exclaimed.

'A secret hamlet whose access is through the legendary gardens, yes. But while everyone knows Vrindavan the gardens, famed for their soma wine, only a few trusted souls know of this secret place. We use the term Vrindavan, but even if the enemy searches the garden for weeks, his armies will not find the way to our secret hamlet.'

Yashoda was reassured even more and began to look forward to seeing the hamlet that her husband had described in such loving terms. After all, Gokuldham had been her home since marriage, while it had been Nanda's since birth. If he looked forward to moving to this new place so enthusiastically, she would not say or do anything to discourage him henceforth.

And so it was on a bright spring day, with a spring in their step and smiles on their lips, that the Vrishnis migrated out of Vrajbhoomi, making the journey to Vrindavan. They travelled by uks wagon carts, horses, mules, even elephants and camels. Helped by the young children, the dogs drew smaller carts of belongings. The long, gaily clad procession was joyful and happy as it made its way across Vraj's meandering hill slopes so that it seemed more like people going to a festival than a migration into exile.

Kaand III

one

The sound of the flute filled the valley. Its haunting melody curled around the senses, evoked forgotten memories and lost emotions, and cleansed the heart of anxiety. In her new home overlooking the lake, Yashoda sang a plaintive folk song to the melody of the flute.

In the meadows, where the vast herds grazed, Nanda and the other Vrishni lords marvelled at how much their yield had increased and health improved. The gopas and gopis who had begun living in the secret hamlet worked and played, loved and lived with renewed hope and vigour. Contrary to their fears, the migration had improved their lot. They had found everything to their liking in this place. The landscape was breathtakingly beautiful, the water clear as crystal, the air sweet, the animals and birds curious and unafraid – itself an auspicious sign – and all omens and signs were favourable in the extreme. The cows were yielding richer, creamier and more milk than ever, curds set perfectly and in less time, buttermilk tasted invigorating and ghee heavenly, and the wine was, of course, superior! But most of all, they felt safe. Not only did the Usurper not know of this place, there was only one ingress point, and it was closely watched night and day by sentries posted in discreet lookout posts. Not one horseman or foot soldier could come to Vrindavan without word reaching Nanda at once; and for an army it would be sheer folly since the ingress point offered an impenetrable defence.

The Vrishnis were happy here, and the sound of the flute expressed their happiness more eloquently than words. That lilting melody, so remarkable, so sweetly sad, so profoundly moving, summed up all the struggle and travails they had gone through as well as the joy they now felt.

They would bide their time here until the Slayer arose. Until the Usurper lay dead. Until Mathura was restored to its rightful ruler.

They would live out their lives, herd their cows, collect their milk, churn their buttermilk, perform their rituals, celebrate their festivals and play the sweet–sad drama of life under these stars and this sky, and bide their time till they were called upon to do whatever was needed.

Warriors all, they had not come here to hide or escape persecution; they had come to grow and strengthen their resolve, and incidentally, defy Mathura by not paying any more taxes. So long as they had remained in Vrajbhoomi, they were obliged to pay the mandatory taxes, and it had galled them all these years to know that those spears and swords and lances borne by the marauding armies of Kamsa were paid for with their own hard-earned coin. Now, by leaving Vraj, they had ended that relationship. This secret vale of Vrindavan was not officially under Mathura's dominion. The Vrishnis owed no one taxes here. The same process was being repeated all across the Yadava nation, for if there was one way to hurt a kingdom, it was by denying it taxes. Without taxes, even the mightiest army would run out of supplies, or motivation, sooner or later. In its own way, this defiance was more effective than open civil revolt and it had the benefit of not costing Yadava lives.

The flute summed up all these things and more – the defiance of the Vrishnis, the tyranny of the Usurper, the heaven-assured coming of the Slayer in time, the end of the reign of evil, the beginning of a new era of hope and peace.

The flute sang on, and in its bittersweet notes was contained the soul of all who now inhabited Vrindavan, for it was from their hearts that Krishna drew these emotions and translated them into song, a song which he then imbued with life through the simple reed length of the flute.

The odd thing was, even when one could see Krishna engaged in other pastimes, one could still hear the song of the flute. It was as if his presence itself called the flute song into being. He had no need to actually touch the flute to his lips and blow: the flute song was the song of his own heart, expressing all that he had come to know about his people.

Right now, though, Krishna was busy with another instrument quite different from a flute.

Balarama and he were sitting by the lake, slinging pebbles across the water. They were attempting to make the pebbles skip on the surface of the lake, but by shooting them from slingshots, not by hand.

'There!' Balarama cried in triumph as his shot skipped twice and almost a third time before sinking into the still surface. 'I did it!'

'Once doesn't count, Bhaiya,' Krishna said calmly, preparing to throw.

'It skipped twice!' Balarama said.

'Once.'

'Twice!'

Krishna slung his pebble. It skipped twice and then sank, almost exactly as the one flung by Balarama. 'There! Now *that's* how you do it.'

'Mine skipped twice and then almost once more. Yours only skipped twice.'

Krishna grinned at his brother. 'Do it again and prove it.' It was his favourite comeback: whenever Balarama claimed to have outdone Krishna, which was almost all the time, Krishna challenged him to do it again.

Balarama promptly loaded a new pebble, wound the sling, then released the shot. The pebble skipped once, twice ... and a third time before making a fourth ripple and sinking into the water.

'There!' Balarama cried excitedly. 'That was at least thrice, maybe even four.'

'Thrice,' said Krishna affecting a bored tone.

'Thrice, then,' Balarama said, folding his arms across his chest. He was twice Krishna's size, weight and width. 'Bet you can't match that.'

Krishna smiled to himself and slung a new pebble. But at the very instant when he was about to fling it, the sound of a calf sounded behind them. Krishna released the pebble but it sank at once with barely a ripple.

Balarama turned in response to the calf's cry. 'What was that?' he said.

For the moment in which Balarama's head was turned, Krishna gestured and the pebble that had sunk rose up again from the water and skipped gaily across the water.

'Now *that's* how you do it,' said Krishna coyly.

Balarama turned back to the lake and saw the line of ripples spreading across the water. 'Seven ... eight?' he cried out, as the pebble finally sank – or was allowed to sink. 'That's impossible! You must have cheated, Krishna!'

Krishna wagged an admonishing finger. 'Don't be a sore loser, Bhaiya. You can try again as many times as you wish. But first let's go see what ails that calf.'

In a bid to curtail their mischief-mongering, Krishna and Balarama had been given charge of the calves. The suggestion had come from Nanda, who had some experience with mischievous children. 'My brothers and I raised hell in Gokul when we were growing up,' he admitted to Yashoda one night. She was surprised. Nanda was so dignified, calm, almost phlegmatic, it was hard to think of him as a snotty-nosed boy running around half-naked in the dust with his brothers, causing mayhem. Yet the stories he told her were hair-raising and blood-curdling, and she prayed aloud that her Krishna and Balarama would not repeat some of the same stunts. And in order to avoid giving her little rascal any ideas, she even made Nanda promise aloud that he would not repeat them in Krishna's presence. Nanda chuckled and promised her. Then he suggested that they let Krishna and Balarama manage the calves.

'Those two rapscallions?' she retorted. 'They'll drive the poor little ones into the water and dance on their backs playing the flute!'

For an instant, Nanda actually imagined Krishna and Balarama dancing on the backs of the poor submerged calves as they lowed and protested noisily. Then he shook his head. 'You might be surprised. Sometimes the best way to curb mischief is to give a naughty child responsibility.'

'Isn't that a contradiction?' she asked. 'Shouldn't responsible chores be given to well-behaved children?'

He shrugged. 'Of course, but even the naughtiest children do grow out of their mischievous ways in time. And one way to help them do that is to give them responsibilities early. I think what our two rascals need is something useful to do, something that takes up just enough of their attention and energy to keep them from getting into mischief all the time. Oh, they won't stop altogether; don't expect miracles overnight. But it is hard to be frolicking and running around when you have a herd of calves to watch over and bring back at end of day.'

Yashoda was doubtful about the idea but agreed to it if only to see if Nanda was right. 'The only thing that worries me,' she said thoughtfully, 'is those poor calves!'

Nanda chuckled. 'My dearest one, you will find that our little dark lord and his brother will be gentler with those poor calves than all the other children in Gokul—' he corrected himself, 'in Vrindavan, I mean.'

She nodded, but her brow remained furrowed.

Krishna and Balarama sprinted up the hillside. All the calves had been on this hillside, around the lake, just a little while ago. And now they seemed to have trooped uphill. But why? There was water on the slope of the lakeside, fresh green grass ... There was no reason for them to trudge uphill suddenly.

They saw the reason as they reached the top of the hill. One of the calves appeared to have gone mad. It was running from one end of the pasture to the other, head-butting its fellow calves, driving them farther away from the lakeside. The other calves were crying out in protest but moving in the direction they were being herded. The mad calf was galloping like a manic horse rather than a young cow, rearing up and kicking backwards and snorting angrily.

'What's got into Gauri 56?' asked Balarama. Since almost all cows were given the same handful of names, Krishna and he had decided that they would attach numbers to the names of the cows to distinguish between the various namesakes. Gauri, literally meaning white-face or fair, was one of the most common names for cows since Vraj cows tended to be white and brown in patches.

Krishna narrowed his eyes. 'That's not Gauri 56,' he said quietly, in an odd tone. 'It's not one of our calves at all.'

Balarama frowned. 'Whose is it, then?'

Krishna turned and looked at him sharply. Balarama looked at his brother's eyes and saw the blue sky reflected in them. Then he realized that what he was seeing was not blue sky at all, but simply the colour blue. The whites of Krishna's eyes had turned deep blue. And something blazed deep within his black pupils, like a banked fire smouldering.

'Uh oh,' Balarama said, recognizing that look. 'Here be asuras.'

And then, in the wink of an eye, Krishna was gone. Balarama felt a faint breeze as his brother shot away, but neither saw Krishna's body blurring, nor his passage from the hill to the meadow below. It was as if Krishna had vanished from this spot and reappeared there – one of the many things Krishna could do but Balarama couldn't.

'Not fair,' Balarama grumbled. 'You always do that!'

He sprinted downhill, compelled to cover the same ground in a more mortal manner, by running fast. But he could see that he would not reach in time to actually do much. That was why Krishna had used that particular means of travel: to put himself in harm's way first and protect his brother. That was what he always did.

'Not fair,' Balarama grumbled again as he ran downhill, gathering speed. '*I'm* the elder brother. *I'm* supposed to take care of you!'

Krishna smelt the demon. It was an oddly pleasant odour – sweetish, slightly milky. Even if he had not possessed preternatural instincts, he would have guessed something was amiss with this particular calf. Real calves never smelt sweet. They stank of dried cow dung, stale milk and half-chewed cud which they often vomited. Those were the smells he associated with them, and for which he loved them. They were the smells of nature, of life itself, of eating and defecating and growing. This odour from the demoniac calf was too unnatural, too perfumed to be real. Only a demon would try to make itself alluring. Real calves were too busy surviving and didn't care to impress anyone!

But if the demon calf had intended to lure Krishna somehow, it was doing a poor job of it. Right now, all it seemed intent on doing was herding the calves in the south-western direction. Why? Krishna watched as the demon calf roared and reared up on its hind legs, before dropping down on the ground with a thud and lowering its head threateningly, all the time exuding fire from its nostrils. Terrified, the calves were running now, beginning to stampede in panic. This appeared to be what the demon calf wanted: to stampede the calves in that direction. What purpose would that serve?

The demon calf turned to face Krishna. It was grinning. There was no other way to describe the look on its bovine features: its lips were curled, revealing big white cow teeth, and its ears were twitching madly though there wasn't a fly in sight. It stamped its fore hooves on the ground, challenging him, then lowered its head, snorting flames from its nostrils.

It meant to charge at him.

Krishna had no issue with that. He would have charged at the demon anyway.

But the calf herd was stampeding madly, already several hundred yards away and running faster. The demon calf had made them panic for a reason, he knew. It could have torn them to pieces, killed several if it wished before Krishna reached and stopped it. Instead, all it wanted was to send the calves running.

Suddenly, Krishna knew why.

'Balarama!' he shouted. 'Stop the calves!'

He felt a rush of air pass by and saw the blurring fair body of his brother go racing past. Balarama could not travel as Krishna could, but he could run very fast when he cared to, and he was running his fastest now. Krishna felt a surge of relief. Thank the goddess he had Balarama with him. Otherwise, he would have been forced to choose between fighting the demon calf and saving the calves.

Now, he could concentrate on the demon calf.

'Come on,' he shouted at the calf, which was still stamping its feet and snorting fire. 'Come on, then.'

The calf lunged forward, coming at him at an all-out run, its head lowered. As it came, horns sprouted instantly from its head. Not the usual two, but a whole thorn-thicket of them, twisted, pointed, razor-edged horns such as nature never produced, each one deadly enough to rip flesh and tear skin to shreds. As it neared Krishna, the horns continued to grow blurringly fast, as long as swords now, then as long as spears, and still growing. Evidently, they were supposed to keep growing even as they struck the enemy and ravaged his body. So that was this demon's 'thing'.

Krishna roared and spread his arms, as if preparing to embrace a friend.

The calf demon crashed into his belly, the horns piercing his body in a dozen places and punching through his flesh and skin and bone. The calf demon roared its triumph and pounded over the ground where Krishna stood.

Balarama sped after the calf herd. At first, even he did not understand Krishna's concern. Then he thought about the direction in which they were racing and understood at once.

There was a gulch in that direction. Twenty or twenty-five yards deep, and lined with sharp rocks and thorny scrub at the bottom. If the calves continued their stampede, they would certainly tumble over the edge and fall into the gulch, killing or maiming every last one of them. So that had been the demon calf's intention. Devilishly clever. And mean. To slaughter an entire herd of innocent calves just to distract Krishna.

But the demon calf had not counted on Krishna having an ally equally capable of fighting – or helping.

Balarama overtook the stampeding herd on the far right side. He blurred past the calves, glancing to his left to see startled white-eyed bovine faces turned down in terror. To the calves, the demon calf had been their worst fear realized. A predator who looked just like one of them. Any animal would have startled them, but it was the shock of seeing one of their own behave that way that had driven them to panic so quickly and easily.

Balarama was ahead of the herd now, and could see the gulch only a few dozen yards ahead. It would be very close. With one final burst of speed, he cut inwards, in front of the stampeding herd. He heard the leaders low in protest but they kept heading straight on. They were by now boxed in by the large boulders that strewed the field and could only make a turn gradually. He would not be able to turn them aside, away from harm's way. The only way was … straight! And that meant he had only one option.

He reached what seemed like a good spot and quickly pushed the boulders on either side inwards, blocking the way ahead until only a narrow passage was left. Just about room for a half dozen head of calves to pass through. He stationed himself in this passage between the boulders and spread his legs, raising his hands, bracing himself for the oncoming stampede.

The first calves struck his outstretched hands with terrific impact. They were not full-grown, but then again, neither was he. It took all his strength and will to keep from being knocked off his feet and trampled over. He held his ground as calf after calf piled up against the leaders, their combined weight and momentum pushing him backwards, his feet skidding in the grassy dirt as he was shoved backwards. He dared not turn his head to see how far he was from the edge but knew it could not be more than a few yards now. And the calf herd still pushed – pushed madly.

Balarama clung on frantically, fighting now not just for the lives of the calves but his own as well. For, if he fell into that gulch now, he would have a hundred head of half-grown cows falling on top of him – and he had no desire to know what that might do to him.

Krishna felt the calf demon's vicious horns ripping through his skin and flesh. He felt the pain that he would have felt had he been merely mortal. He also felt the fiery sensation that was more than any mortal could have felt. That was specially for him. Some kind of asura poison that only affected devas and their amsas or avatars. He felt the demon's exhilaration at having accomplished his mission. He even read the calf demon's thoughts.

'Lord of asuras be praised! I have done what even mighty Putana and Trnavarta could not accomplish! I have slain the Slayer! I shall be richly rewarded for this. A hundred Brahmins shall I feast on tonight once my lord rewards my success.'

Krishna focussed his energy on the parts of his body that had been torn and damaged by the asura's horns and poison. He felt the milk of Ananta seeping through him, culled from the ethereal realm of vaikuntha, felt it healing, repairing, rebuilding. Within moments, his mortal body was whole again, as undamaged and unblemished as it had been before the calf demon's charge.

'Not so fast,' he said aloud to the demon. 'You have to finish your mission before you get to feast.'

The calf demon had raced past him after goring his body. Now, it swung around, hooves kicking up sods of earth and clods of grassy mud as it turned its bovine body. Its large cow eyes bulged as it looked at little Krishna, still standing, arms akimbo, untouched.

'But … I gored you!' it cried out in anger and frustration. 'I felt the flesh rip! I saw your blood splatter. I sensed your vile mortal smell.'

'Yes,' Krishna said, the blue of his whites now expanding to fill the entire well of his eye sockets, his black pupils disappearing to tiny pinpoints within an ocean of deep blue, the blue glow spilling out from his eyes, flashing out like liquid light to extend for yards around him, like the light of a lamp in darkness. 'Now see my non-mortal side.'

And this time he charged the calf demon, roaring and lowering his head.

The beast had not admitted defeat yet. With a bellow of fury, it lowered its head and lurched forward, combining the little boy's momentum with its own furious charge.

Child and calf met in a collision so resounding that birds fell stunned from trees, fish held still in the lake, and all across Vrindavan, every Vrishni heard the sound and looked up at the sky, mistaking it for a clap of thunder.

Balarama heard the sound too, but was too busy to pay heed to it. The first of the herd had struck him at almost the same instant, and he was using all his considerable strength to act as a wall. The calves crashed into each other one after the other, their forward momentum driving the whole group forward, each impact pushing Balarama's feet inches backward – towards the yawning gorge. He knew that he had already been pushed several yards past the boulders he had hurriedly shoved together. Which meant he must be close … He felt the back of one foot grappling for purchase, meeting only empty air.

Another calf, a laggard, struck the back of the herd. Balarama bellowed with strain as he pushed back, shoving with all his might. The struggle he underwent was not merely one of strength, but one of size too. Powerfully endowed though he was with supernatural energy – the strength of the eternal serpent himself, as well as a portion of Vishnu's own energies – he was limited by his human form. And right now, that form was the body of a little boy. As it was, his hands were raised up to their limit, holding the snout of one calf and the hump of another, and his little feet were scraping for a hold on the gritty ground. He roared again, not merely restraining now, but actively pushing forward.

The calf herd lowed and called out in protest as the younguns felt their hooves being pushed backwards and they began slipping back over the ground, digging furrows in the earth.

'Back!' Balarama yelled. 'Back, you idiots!'

Something of his intent must have communicated itself to the herd, or perhaps his shoving tipped them off. Either way, they began to turn head and move back the way they had come. They milled about in confusion, unsure which way to go to escape from the danger.

'Back, you fools!' Balarama said as he slapped the last of them away from him. He took a moment or two to catch his breath and wipe the sweat from his brow.

Only then did he turn and look back ... no, directly down at the gorge, right under his feet.

three

After counting every last head of the herd to ensure that none had run off or been harmed, Krishna and Balarama regrouped by the lake. For once, they also looked at each calf's snout, just to ensure that none were calf demons mingled with the rest, biding their time. One of the older calves, a female, opened her mouth and gave Balarama a good look at a mouthful of half-chewed cud before spitting it out at him.

'Thank you,' he said quietly, wiping off the mess without malice, 'but I'm not hungry right now.'

He patted her neck affectionately, proud of the fact that he had not lost a single one.

'That wasn't so bad,' he said, turning back to Krishna. Then stopped.

Krishna was staring at the lake.

Balarama looked. He could see nothing out of the ordinary. Just the lake, the trees, creepers, vines, flowers, birds, a few kraunchya with their thin legs in the shallows, dipping their long beaks in search of fish.

'What is it, Brother?' he asked, puzzled.

Krishna inclined his head slightly. 'Demons,' he said. 'I can still smell them.'

Balarama frowned. What did that 'still' mean? Krishna hadn't mentioned smelling any in the first place. Oh wait, he remembered Krishna saying something about keeping their eyes open and their senses alert the very day they came to Vrindavan. But that had been a while ago. Nothing untoward had happened since then. Balarama had come to think that perhaps they would be able to spend their time in play in the bountiful place. He liked the place just as much as his mother Rohini did. He liked the fact that she was happy here. It made him happy as well. But Krishna had been acting different ever since they had arrived. He was not as mischievous as before, nor as radical in his pranks and tricks. It was as if he had been waiting. Waiting for what?

Waiting for this. For the asuras to emerge and show themselves. And attack.

And it seemed that day had come.

Krishna knew the demon was close by. But he could not tell where it was or in what form. All he could do was wait for it to show itself.

He watched the lake, glad that Balarama was standing quietly beside him. Balarama-bhaiya could sometimes ask too many questions or talk too much.

Everything seemed normal. Birds landed in the trees and took off. Monkeys chittered and leapt from branch to branch. The fish swam in the lake, creating ripples below the surface. The kraunchya birds hopped slowly from foot to foot, seeking prey. One of the kraunchyas was coming out of the water on to the lake shore. The commotion of the calf demon's attack had passed, and nature had returned to its usual equanimity.

Krishna glanced back at the hilltop. The calf demon's attack had taken place on the other side. He had destroyed it in the second charge, ripping its body to shreds, snapping each length of horn to fragments; then he had buried the demon deep within the ground. He had come to the lake afterwards, to slake his thirst and wash the offal off his body. Now, the calf herd grazed peacefully in its usual hillside spot and all seemed well.

But he knew the demon was close. He could smell it. It seemed closer now, if anything! But where was it? There was nothing but the kraunchya on the lake shore in front of him.

One of the cranes raised its wings and flapped them once, opening and closing its long beak. It seemed to be complaining to Krishna about the lack of fish.

Krishna turned to Balarama. 'We should take the herd back.'

'Already?' Balarama glanced at the sky. 'There's plenty of time yet. The other boys will have finished their chores and will come by to play with us here as usual. They always help us herd the calves back.'

'Don't argue with me, Bhaiya,' little Krishna said to his brother who was twice as large, tall and wide as he. 'We should take the herd home now and warn the other children not to come by the lakeside today. We can always—'

'KRISHNA!' Balarama yelled.

Krishna swung around, just in time to see an enormous gaping maw converge upon him. The gigantic maw enfolded him completely, and some giant creature swallowed him whole.

Balarama could barely comprehend what he had seen. One moment there was nothing dangerous in sight. Then suddenly a giant maw had converged on Krishna – and swallowed him up in a trice! Only now, after it happened, did he see that the thing that had swallowed Krishna was the very kraunchya that had been on the lake shore nearby. The crane had suddenly come running up the gradually sloping incline of the lake shore towards where they had been standing, expanding in size as it came. In a trice, it was ten times the size of a normal kraunchya. Now the crane loomed above him, thrashing about, its elongated beak shut tightly, emitting peculiar sounds. The other kraunchya birds in the lake reacted to the appearance of this abnormal fellow and sent up raucous cries of alarm and distress. They took to the air one by one and flew away, calling out their shock at seeing one of their own behave thus. Other birds reacted as well, rising in hordes from the trees and nearby thickets and groves, each calling out in their own unique voices, indignantly protesting this intrusion into their peaceful hamlet.

Balarama stared up at the enormous crane circling in front of him. It appeared to be dancing about, its webbed feet thudding down on the ground as it hopped. One foot landed very close to him and he realized that he ought to get out of its way. But Krishna! The wretched thing had swallowed Krishna! Had he not seen it happen with his own eyes, he would never have believed it. He had been looking directly at his little brother when the cursed crane had come bounding up like a dog and swallowed him in its giant beak.

'Balarama!' cried a chorus of voices. 'Krishna!'

He turned just as the children of Vrindavan came racing over the hilltop. It was time for them to play until the sun dipped lower and they had to shepherd the calves home. They came over the rise and started running downhill, waving and yelling at him. He saw their eyes go wide, showing the whites, and their pace slow, their arms cease waving and their mouths gape open when they saw what was going on by the lake – a giant kraunchya hopping about angrily, making bizarre animalistic sounds, while Balarama moved about trying to avoid being crushed by its giant webbed feet.

The children screamed and yelled, pointing to the giant bird. Yet, despite their horror, they still came on, unable to wholly comprehend what they were witnessing. Balarama tried to raise his hands and shouted to wave them off.

'Go back home! It's a demon! It has swallowed Krishna!'

Dhum! The bird's foot narrowly missed hitting him.

He looked up, more concerned now with his own survival than with waving the other children away. They should be able to see the danger for themselves, after all.

The kraunchya was growing more and more agitated. It was doing everything but fly – flapping its wings, opening its beak wide to emit a bizarre parody of the natural crane bird cry, hopping about from foot to foot.

Suddenly, it screamed with agony and shuddered. It came to a dead halt, beak raised to the sky, entire body taut and quivering. It shuddered again. And again.

Balarama saw something occur around the throat of the bird demon. A discolouration. The white feathers there were turning dark bluish, as if dark blue blood were seeping from within it, staining its pristine ivory plumage. But he doubted that asuras had blue blood – green perhaps, but surely not blue. Blue was the colour of Brahman, the infinite force of which the whole of Creation was composed, the colour of dharma and devas. No. That discolouration could only mean one thing: Krishna. His brother might have been swallowed whole by the demon in a moment of ingenious ambush, but swallowing was not the same as digesting. No mere demon could simply consume

Krishna! And that colour spreading like blood across the porcelain plumage of the bird demon was proof of it. Krishna's presence in the bird's throat was causing it more discomfort than a burning coal. A flaming coal of pure Brahman energy incarnate in human form.

That, my friend, Balarama thought with pride, *is my brother. Swallow that, demon!*

With a final shuddering croak, the kraunchya demon bent its long neck, pointing its beak at the ground, and heaved once, twice, thrice. With the third heave came a great outrush, and Balarama winced, raising a hand to cover his face in case the demon had been performing its role as a crane too diligently. He didn't mind cow froth or even cow dung, but half-digested fish he could do without!

To his relief, the only thing that fell from the giant beak was a familiar little form – two legs, two hands, two eyes ... Yes, Krishna – intact and fully operational. Back on earth!

Their playmates yelled and shouted in wonderment, pointing. Balarama glanced back and saw that several of them had come within yards of where he stood. The fools! Did they not realize the danger they were in? If it had been one of them that the bird demon had swallowed, he would have been half through the creature's digestive system by now, slowly putrefying. He began to yell at them again, but just then Krishna rose to his feet and leapt up in the air.

The kraunchya demon had still not fully recovered after regurgitating Krishna. Clearly, having the child-god in his throat had not suited its physiognomy. The blue stain around its throat remained even now, as if irreparable harm had been caused to that region.

Now, as Krishna leapt up, the demon screeched and paddled its feet backwards. But Krishna was too quick for it. With one deft move, he grasped hold of its beak, the upper in one hand and the lower in the other.

The demon cawed and fell sideways in its attempt to escape. Its legs and wings thrashed about helplessly.

Krishna stood on the lower beak, almost sideways now, and pushed the two beaks apart with all his might. As he pushed, he expanded himself, growing as rapidly as the crane demon itself had grown before ambushing him. In the wink of an eye, he was as large as the demon itself, and the creature's beaks were pushed to their farthest point and beyond.

The bird demon issued one final chilling cry which echoed through the valley. Then, a horrible tearing sound followed as Krishna pushed its beaks apart past the breaking point. Balarama averted his eyes.

four

The children danced around Krishna and Balarama, hands interlinked, chanting songs praising Vishnu. The elders were gathered in the village communal centre, at the top of the meadow where Nanda's herds grazed. They glanced at Krishna several times, then at each other. None knew what to say next.

It was Gargamuni who came to their rescue with the right words. The preceptor had accompanied them into exile, insisting that their spiritual welfare was his responsibility. He was also their sole contact with the outside world now, since he could come and go freely without anyone daring to question his movements or motives.

'It is time to acknowledge the truth, Nanda Maharaja,' said the old sage, his light brown eyes twinkling in the golden light of sunset. 'And it is time for all to know the reason why your son has survived every attack by the most formidable demons imaginable. He has done what no grown man could have done each time, and he has done it over and over again. Indeed,' Gargamuni paused dramatically, 'he has done what no mortal could have.'

Everyone looked at him in awe. Even those who had suspected or dreamed or sensed what he was about to say next had never thought the day would come when it would be acknowledged and asserted in so many words. Yet when the great Brahmin who was their spiritual and religious guide himself spoke the words aloud, each and every person present there knew at once that he spoke the absolute undeniable truth. They knew this in the same way that any living creature on earth can recognize the sun in the sky, the life-giver of all natural things, for all living beings recognize their benefactor as all babes know their birth-mother.

'He is swayam Bhagwan, sent to grace us and live amongst us. He is the great soul, the fount of Brahman itself, father of Brahma the Creator and originator of worlds infinite. *He is the Slayer of Kamsa.*'

Then the great Brahmin grew melancholy and sad, falling silent until Nanda asked him gently what the matter was. 'Alas,' said Gargacharya, 'now it is certain that Krishna's presence here is known to all those who serve the purpose of evil. Even if Kamsa himself dare not set foot in this vale to challenge our beloved deva just yet, he will surely send out a horde of demons. I fear that the asuras in the form of the crane bird and the calf were only the beginning. The assault on Krishna will be unending now, and ever-escalating. It is no less than a war. Except that this war is waged upon a single being, this little son of Vasudeva and Devaki.' By this time, the guru had told the whole story of the Slayer's birth and the people gathered were aware of every last detail of Krishna's extraordinary conception, birth and true origins.

'What can we do to help our saviour in this fight?' asked someone.

'Yes,' added another voice that was echoed by all present. 'If need be, we are willing to lay down our lives for him. For he is the one we have been waiting for, our salvation. We shall protect him by all means.'

Garga shook his head sadly. 'Your sentiments are sincere, but your efforts would be of no avail. The Slayer must walk this path alone. This is a testing time for him. It is his karma to battle the demons sent by Kamsa and his evil allies single-handedly.'

'But he will surely prevail, will he not?' asked a hesitant voice. This was none other than Yashoda.

Garga turned a kind but troubled face to her.

'Would that I could say yes without doubt, good Yashoda. But the truth is that these things are not the province of us mere mortals. All I can say is that if the answer was such a foregone conclusion, there would be no fight, no struggle. Our Lord in this child's form would simply go forth and destroy the Usurper and liberate us all from his tyranny. That he does not do so indicates that he is not ready yet. Perhaps he requires time to grow his physical body. Perhaps he needs to perform some other mystical dharma of which we are not aware. Perhaps he simply needs to face these challenges and prove himself before he is ready to face the lord of these demons and fulfil the prophecy. I cannot say for certain. All I can say is that even a prophecy is but a prediction, and even a god can be defeated, even killed. I say this not to frighten you, good mother, but merely because those who know Brahman can never be untruthful. It would violate my vows. Since you asked the question, I must answer honestly. And this is my honest answer: Krishna must survive these tasks and challenges on his own. That is all I can say for now.'

Everyone was silent, pondering over the words of the preceptor. Outside, in the fading light of dusk, the children continued to play. In the centre stood Krishna on one foot, his other foot bent in his favourite stance – head tilted, chin pointed upwards – playing his flute.

The melody drifted across the whole of Vrindavan, and in the distant woods, leaves stirred, as if roused by an invisible wind, and strange sounds – from creatures that were omnipresent but which none could see – startled the gentler denizens of the woods.

Deep in the darkling woods and thickets, where the wormwood crumbled, laughter echoed, mocking the music.

And the flute played on.

The Krishna–Kamsa Conflict
Concludes In

LORD OF MATHURA

Book 4 of The Krishna Coriolis

Coming soon!

acknowledgements

R. Sabarish, my first reader, who read the first drafts of this version back in 2005 when it was still a part of my larger Mba (Mahabharata) retelling, and who shall probably be reading this published version on a different continent now – an achievement that suggests that perhaps I have managed in some way to keep the flame of our epics burning brightly after all. Thank you, Sabs!

Tapas Sadasivan Nair, who read through the final draft of the first two books in the Krishna Coriolis Series years before publication and suggested many valuable corrections and amendments. If not the first, certainly one of my best readers and whose feedback I value greatly. Read on, Kanjisheikh!

For the members of my erstwhile Epic India Group, Forums and the 33,000+ (and counting) readers who have left their wonderful reviews, comments and feedback on my blog at ashokbanker.com over the years. Too many now to name, so I'll settle for ululating without the benefit of a vuvuzela: 'EI! EI! YO!' Proud 2B an Epicindian. Always hamesha forever!

V.K. Karthika, who has turned out to be the editor and publisher who has shown the most faith and support for my work in my entire career, readily buying more books from me, trusting my instincts and giving me whatever was needed to enable the completion of this massively ambitious work. The interesting thing is that Karthika and I first connected not as author and editor, even though we knew each other as acquaintances for years, but as readers sharing a common interest in fantasy, romance and historical sagas. I think that's what makes her such a great editor to work with: she actually reads and enjoys the books she publishes, which is not something I can say for all editors working in publishing today. I am truly grateful for her enduring support and enthusiasm for my work. Karthika, I hope to continue publishing with you for decades to come.

Prema Govindan, whom I didn't even know by name when she turned in the first set of edits on the manuscript of this book, but whose great love for the subject of this book, Krishna, coupled with an intense professional drive to bring out the best book possible and the rare ability to appreciate an author's individual (and very quirky) 'voice' or style – including my penchant for mixing languages, cultures, et al. in an epic khichdi – resulted in the best editing of my career. And since the first book, I have now had the pleasure of working with her on two more books in the series, the experience turning out to be just as rewarding. Prema, it has been a great pleasure and I hope to have your eagle eye and keen mind on every single book in this series and possibly many more as well.

The entire team at HarperCollins India – too many to name, yet each one a star in his or her own right – that is responsible for bringing this book to you, the reader holding this copy in your hands, aided and abetted by the distributors, stockists, retailers and other book trade professionals across the country who are helping the book publishing business defy recessions and break global records. Thank you, all!

As always, my family, starting with my beloved wife Bithika, my daughter Yashka, my son Ayush, and my constant companion

Willow, whose love and support are the fountainhead of my life and work. Our story is the one story that I can never hope to better! Love, always.

And finally, you, dear reader, whether you're new to my work or a long-time familiar. If you've never read anything by me before, you should know that I approach every book as if it's my first and only book – never expect the same thing twice because I don't write the same book twice. And if you've read every single thing I've written to date, you probably know that already, in which case, you won't be surprised when you turn the page and find that this book and series is quite unlike everything else I've written before. But what really matters is that you like reading it as much as I loved writing it.

Because I really did. That, and that alone, is the reason why I wrote it. Because I love writing.

And love, like most communicable viruses, is extremely contagious, though thankfully not as harmful to your health.

ASHOK KUMAR BANKER

Andheri, Mumbai
November 2011

Govinda has been weaving his magic since before
he was born in …

SLAYER OF KAMSA

Book 1 of The Krishna Coriolis

Cowherd, lover, warrior, god incarnate. The youthful superhero of ancient India is here …

Forewarned by a prophecy, the demonic Prince Kamsa orders every male newborn to be put to the sword. But even in the womb, Krishna uses powerful magic to cast a spell across the entire kingdom on the night of his birth. Now, the stage is set for the epic clash of the child-god and the terrible forces of evil with the birth of Krishna, the slayer of Kamsa …

The fantastic adventures of the Hindu god Krishna have entertained and inspired people for millennia. Playful cowherd, mischievous lover, feared demon-slayer – the legendary exploits of this super-being in human form rival the most rousing fantasy epics. Now, the author of the Ramayana Series®, the hugely successful epic retelling of the ancient Sanskrit poem, works his magic once again with the tales of Krishna. All the pomp, splendour and majesty of ancient India come alive in this extraordinary eight-book series.

Govinda has been dancing on, through many more action-packed adventures in …

DANCE OF GOVINDA

Book 2 of The Krishna Coriolis

Govinda, god-child, redeemer of the world, takes on the might of Kamsa

As we move into the second instalment of Ashok K. Banker's Krishna tales, the prophesied Slayer of Kamsa has been born and smuggled out of Mathura in the dead of night. Kamsa finds that his nephew has escaped and flies into a demoniac rage. Meanwhile, his ally Jarasandha of Magadha arrives in Mathura with his coterie of powerful supporters to ensure that Kamsa stays loyal to him. But Kamsa is not to be crushed. With the help of Putana, a powerful demoness living incognito among humans, he slowly regains his strength and acquires new powers.

Packed with surprising insights into the characters of Kamsa and Putana, *Dance of Govinda* is a brilliant interpretation of the nature of evil in a world that teeters on the edge of violence.